NEMESIS OF THE GODS

Hera Greek Myths Retold Book Three

Ava McKevitt

SAPERE
BOOKS

NEMESIS OF THE GODS

Published by Sapere Books.

24 Trafalgar Road, Ilkley, LS29 8HH

saperebooks.com

ISBN: 978-0-85495-553-4

For Christopher, who first showed me how to write and then how to create worlds.

1: GANYMEDE

The greatest war of our age was not born from hate but from love. Since Homer first sang the songs of the *Iliad* and the *Odyssey*, the tale of the Trojan War has never been forgotten. It has formed one of the foundations of storytelling on Earth to this day. The poet was a favourite of the Muses and a genius among artists in his skill with rhythms, rhyming, and dialects, so the lyrical tale ebbs and flows with ease and mastery. While so many have re-imagined it, re-telling it from nearly every angle possible, few have caught the world's attention to quite the same extent as Homer. It is one of the most revered stories in the cosmos's long and complicated history for humans and gods alike.

Aristotle once said that through tragic tales, one can be purified of terror and grief — one is allowed to process these emotions in a pretence where the effects do not directly impact one's personal life, just one's imagination; second-hand emotion, if you will. It is why people love stories so much. It is why theatre was created from drama. It is why poetry and song exist and why some dedicated souls sit and read the pages of books in their leisure time. It is also why the tale of Troy continues to capture the imagination. It presents both the wonderful and the horrible while keeping its audience safe and sound. Yet there are layers within Homer's narratives that I plan to tell you, details not yet known, and a new side to this age-old tale of love and glory: mine.

The Trojan War is no small feat to describe, but I shall do my best. Most have been led to believe that the mortals began the hostility. Still, the abduction of Helene of Sparta originated in Olympos, not in the world of men. The resultant war involved houses of great nobility and heritage on both sides of the Aegean Sea, once called the Open Sea. Yet it affected the entirety of Hellas, not just those families or a single city. Its effect spread from the highest peak of the Thrakian mountains in the north beyond Makedonia, down to Krete and beyond in the Great Sea, and from Korkyra in the west to the Hellespont in the east, with all the white islands of the blue Aegean Sea in between them.

The epic story tells of far more than just famous 'heroes', whom mortals have glorified for thousands of years, fighting other noble warriors in front of great walls as a powerful but honourable lord tries to rescue his beautiful wife from her captors while the gods place bets on which side the Moirai — the three sisters of fate — will favour, and then turn the tide of the battle themselves. The whole war is a tale of adventure, heroism, and glory, but also of heinous crimes, horrors, and death. It is filled with rage, rape, revenge, trickery, treachery, political conspiracy, enmity, mercy, love, and valour. Like all wars, the victims were countless. Men, women, and children died not just by the sword on the battlefield but also from cold-hearted murder, suicide, and even cannibalism. So, do not be under any illusion that I will grace those so-called 'heroes' with yet more praise. This is *my* story, not theirs.

I had reached a new low in my marriage, one I had never imagined possible. During the recent Gigantomachy, my husband, Zeus, had allowed the Gigante Porphyrion to attack me. He would have watched him pollute me with no remorse or sympathy. I am convinced I would have been defiled had Herakles not intervened on my behalf. Afterwards, I was in despair for a while. Eventually, I resolved to give up all hope of Zeus's care and compassion for me and to resign myself to the gossip and the hatred of the court. I would be what they wanted me to be, but one day, I promised myself, I would prove them wrong. My hatred of Zeus was at its strongest, and I no longer attended court. I tried to avoid being in the same part of the palace as my husband whenever possible. Instead, I spent my days with my youngest daughter, Eris, waiting for my justice to come.

One day, after calling the entire court to the throne room, including me, my husband announced that he had looked down from Mount Olympos upon the city of Troia, once known as Dardania, where my family had slaved for a year. The city lay in the Troad region of Phrygia, a province within the realm of Anatolia, a place to the east beyond Hellenic borders, across the Aegean Sea. Zeus claimed he had heard of how great a nation it had become, equal to the power of Mykenai in Hellas at that time.

"Indeed, it is a splendid place," Zeus announced. "They have built a magnificent city full of handsome people, ruled by King Tros, who has named the city Troia. However, he does not shine the brightest in the Trojan court, nor his heir Prince Ilus, but his youngest son, Ganymede. I had heard of this youth's rare beauty, the most wondrous known among mortals. This Ganymede has a form so exquisite to behold, I was captivated from the first moment I saw him."

Then Zeus turned to our daughter Hebe, who stood nearby, holding an amphora of wine. "This Ganymede shall be my new cupbearer. You do not mind, do you, Hebe? No doubt, by now you are wishing to turn your attention to your wifely duties after marrying Herakles. No respectable housewife is employed."

Hebe's face fell. Her cheeks flushed bright red, looking away from her father. He was taking from her the only position that she, the goddess of youth, had ever carried out in service to the cosmos and a position so highly valued that it signified complete trust from the king.

I was dumbfounded, staring at my husband from my throne beside him. It was not as if he had thought long and hard. No, he had made the decision because it was easy. He simply waved his hand and got what he wanted, not caring about upsetting those around him, especially his family. Zeus's selfishness never failed to surprise and infuriate me.

Ganymede soon came to court. It was rumoured that Zeus, in the form of an eagle, abducted the youth from Mount Ida, which lay south of Troia, where the Trojan king sent his sons to do humble work before taking up their princely offices.

Upon arrival at Olympos, Zeus held a great feast in his honour. He announced that King Tros had been compensated for losing his third son with two horses so swift that they could run over water. Ganymede was immediately given the gift of a drinking cup to signify his new role as the server to the gods, military attire as a mark of his education to come, and immortality and everlasting youth to keep him beautiful. However, Zeus had been right: Ganymede was truly exceptional in his beauty. Not younger than sixteen, he had shoulder-length, golden locks upon a tall young body of lean muscle. He moved with the grace and elegance expected of a prince. No one could take their eyes off him.

It was clear that from the first day of Ganymede's servitude that Zeus doted on him, wholly besotted. When he stared at Ganymede from across the room, it was no affair of the heart or mind. The youth's appeal was purely physical. I supposed that my husband had begun to feel the effects of the ages. Zeus had become more impatient as he spent his days listening to complaints about how his world was still not good enough, which he could not understand. I suspected he may have been yearning for the time when he had more zeal for ruling the cosmos. This did not mean he wanted to relinquish the throne, but the novelty of it had gone and the tediousness had set in somewhat. So, new faces, beautiful ones like that of Ganymede, refreshed his spirit.

Ganymede's rise to Olympos profoundly affected earthly society as Zeus had now begun an erotic relationship between an older man and a teenage youth. It became a beacon of hope for men attracted to other men. However, for some this was not a desirable cultural progression. For the most part, it was agreed that any free man who desired another free man was publicly shamed, censured like a criminal, although they had committed no crime. Instead, the homosexual relationship had to be pederastic; there always had to be a younger and an older. The more senior party would mentor the younger as an aspect of their relationship, teaching him how to be a man. As for abuses within the relationship, such problems went unaddressed, for those who were the dominant party likely possessed influence elsewhere in society, Zeus most of all.

Meanwhile, Hebe was inconsolable. She kept hoping that Zeus would tire of his new distraction. Not even the affectionate attention of Herakles was enough to cheer her up. She found no joy in the world for the first time in her life, for she had experienced her first rejection from her father. Unfortunately, all she could do was get used to it.

No surprise, I was disgusted by Zeus's infatuation. It was not so much that he desired a mortal or indeed a male youth. It was the public display of infidelity and the dismissal of my daughter which offended me. It was blatant adultery, and there was nothing I could do about it. And so, I despised Ganymede, and made a point to refuse his offers of drinks. As a matter of fact, Ganymede's arrival on Olympos was the first insult which drove me to support the Achaeans in the Trojan War, for it was as if Zeus had announced that his own wife was not beautiful enough for him.

2: ERIS

One day, the Olympian court received a messenger who announced that King Peleus of Phthia was to get married, and the Olympian court was invited to attend the celebrations. The court erupted in delight at the thought of such a merry occasion, including myself, for I was grateful for the distraction. Zeus allowed the gathered assembly to disperse and begin preparations. As everyone ran around the palace fetching their best garments, I do not think that anyone except the Moirai were aware that this happy occasion would breed a new era of bloodshed and set the course of Hellenic foreign affairs for thousands of years.

Walking into the temple on Mount Pelion, on the arm of Zeus, I saw familiar faces, some from Olympos and others from around our extensive empire. The wedding guests bowed and curtseyed in respect at our approach. I moved off Zeus's arm and stood in front of the altar, looking down upon the congregation, ready to carry out my duties as the goddess of marriage.

King Peleus stood off to the side, a tall, dark-haired man with bright blue eyes. He stood with a smirk playing on his lips, a look I knew well, and shared a smug expression with Zeus.

The atmosphere grew quiet when the bride appeared in the doorway to the temple on her father's arm, Nereus, the god of freshwaters. The hall fell so silent that only their footsteps towards the altar could be heard.

I sucked in a breath when I saw the bride. Yes, she was beautiful, but hers was also a face I had hoped never to see again: Thetis. I was unsure what to make of the sight of my old foe in bridalwear walking up the aisle towards me and her husband-to-be.

The years had made Thetis no less beautiful. Her golden hair cascaded down her shoulders, and bright green seaweed had been plaited into tiny braids around her face. Her saffron veil was lined with seashells. Hints of aquamarine thread had been woven into her light blue gown.

Then my eyes flitted down to her swollen belly. I had to bite my tongue to prevent a snort of laughter. Yes, Queen Thetis was positively glowing on her wedding day. One did not need to be the goddess of motherhood to realise she was pregnant.

Her eyes widened when she saw me staring back at her. She glanced nervously at her betrothed as she approached the altar, before casting her eyes to the ground, cheeks red. It evidently had not occurred to her that I — whom she had once tried to supplant as Queen of Heaven — would be presiding over her wedding ceremony.

I relished the sight of her shock and dismay, savouring her humiliation. I glanced between the pair and could tell there was no hope. So, I gave them my sweetest smile. "I am so happy for you both."

Peleus grinned. "Thank you, my lady."

Thetis smiled, but it did not meet her eyes. "Yes, thank you."

Then I carried out my duties with a delight I had not felt in a long time.

After the ceremony, we returned to the palace of Phthia, where Peleus carried his bride over the threshold. Then we gathered in the great hall for music and mirth with food, speeches, laughter, and dancing. Zeus caroused his brother, Poseidon, and his sons. Aphrodite, Athene, Artemis, and Demeter joined the heavenly chorus in their merriment which lasted several nights, not just one. The Muses played their instruments in the corner of the room, and Apollo sang. Meanwhile, Dionysos made sure all the mortal men were drinking their fill.

The royal couple was presented with an array of gifts throughout the celebrations. Cheiron, the wise centaur who lived in a nearby cave, who had a reputation for giving aid and advice to heroes, provided the groom with a spear of ashen wood, the blade forged by my son Hephaistos and the rest polished by Athene. Aphrodite gifted the couple a bowl with the figure of Eros engraved on it. Athene gave them a flute. Nereus, Thetis's father, gave them a basket full of salt, which could cause insatiable greed for food. Zeus granted them wings, which Thetis was to present to her first child. Poseidon brought as his presents the fine stallions Balios and Xanthos. Finally, I gave them a chlamys, a type of woollen cloak that warriors often wore, and bade them give it to their first son.

Deep into the celebrations, sudden shouts erupted from the entrance to the hall.

Eris, my youngest daughter, stood in the doorway.

The image of her father, with a sculpted face and long golden hair, Eris was rather athletic-looking for a maiden. Her hair billowed around her like a wild mane. The goddess of strife glared at those present with stormy grey eyes. She sauntered slowly inside.

All fell silent at her entrance. Even the music stopped.

"What a merry gathering," she sneered, moving past the uncertain faces. "Such an honour it is to be an invitee. Only I would not know."

I rushed to my daughter, pushing through the crowds. "My darling, what brings you here?"

The interruption of wedding festivities did not impress me. I also did not wish for her behaviour to negatively reflect on the royal family. So, I turned to the bride and groom. "You must forgive my daughter's dramatic flair."

"No, no," Thetis said. "She must forgive *us*. We decided not to invite any deity to our wedding who represented any matter of ill-will. Yet now I see the irony. Please accept our most humble apologies, Lady Eris." She seemed sincere enough in her regret.

Eris scowled. She was not in the habit of forgiving easily. She glanced around the room. "Where is my brother?"

"Which one?" I asked, hoping she meant Hephaistos.

"My favourite one," she snapped, scanning the crowd. "Ares."

Ares, of course, was present. He did nothing to control his little sister, with whom he got on so well. Lounging back in a chair at one of the feasting tables, he raised his goblet to her in greeting.

"The god of war is present at your wedding, Queen Thetis," Eris pointed out. "Explain that."

"You are correct, my lady," Peleus said, coming to his new wife's aid. "Forgive me, but Ares is a great god. It would have been a grave insult to exclude him."

My ichor ran cold.

Eris's face darkened. "Am *I* not an Olympian, too?" she spat at them. "Am *I* not great?" Her voice rose to a roar.

The bride and groom's faces paled, their mouths failing to find entreaties.

"Eris, this is not the place —" I began, going to take her hand to lead her away.

"No!" She moved out of my reach. "I shall show you what havoc even the most insignificant god can cause!" she shouted, jabbing a finger at the couple.

She whirled around, heading back towards the door. Before she left, she turned and drew something from beneath her cloak. She revealed a glistening golden apple, held in both hands.

At the sight of it, a collective gasp filled the room.

I stared at it, dumbfounded. I recognised it. It was mine.

"That is from the Garden of the Hesperides." *My garden.*

"Indeed, Mother," Eris cackled.

At first, I was unable to believe she had found my sanctuary. However, later I realised it was not so surprising. Since Herakles found my haven, and his life had become legendary, the world had been made privy to my private glen on the other side of the Great Sea. And so, many had been searching far and wide to seek out its secret location. I realised it had been foolish to think no one would succeed, least of all my own daughter who surpassed most others with her cunning.

She turned to the crowd. "This fruit will only ever belong to one person in this world," she announced, giving it a little kiss. "The most beautiful of the goddesses."

After a moment's silence, the room erupted with noise and chatter. It was clear from the face of every goddess present — even Thetis — that they were each thinking the same thing.

Righteous indignation settled over me. If anyone had a right to the apple, it was me. For I owned its birthplace, and I was the Queen of Olympos. By rank, I was the most beautiful. By right, I was its owner.

Eris tossed the golden apple up into the air, wearing a triumphant grin.

Chaos ensued as each goddess lunged for it, Thetis and me included. Brawling broke out, hair and limbs flying, as we all hit and kicked each other. I gained a few scratches, bites, and bruises, but I also gave a few back.

"Cease this behaviour at once!" a tremendous, booming voice bellowed.

A shiver ran down my spine at the sound of my husband's voice. We released each other, standing apart, dishevelled and ashamed. There was silence.

Fury on his face, Zeus seized the golden apple from the ground. "I shall keep this for now."

Then he turned to Peleus. "I think it is time you took your bride to bed, King of Phthia."

Meekly, Peleus bowed and took his wife's hand, leading her from the room.

"Hera, follow them," Zeus ordered me.

Remembering my duties, I tailed after the couple, finding it difficult to tear myself away from the room where the golden apple was. Yet I had no option but to obey.

Thetis looked over her shoulder at me, alarmed, then seemed to remember the last of my responsibilities as a goddess of marriage: to oversee the consummation.

I looked away from her, blushing.

It was as awkward as I feared. I had turned myself invisible when they entered the bridal chamber. Thetis looked around the room in concern, searching for me. However, Peleus told her to stop worrying, to get undressed, and to get into the bed.

Peleus was rough with his bride, consummating their union unnecessarily, with no apparent regard for her delicate condition. I did not have much care for Thetis herself, but I did not like the thought of her innocent baby being harmed. Thetis, for her part, buried her face in the sheets, not making a sound, and let him do what he wanted. She sat on the bed when he was done, keeping her head lowered. Saying nothing, Peleus redressed and left the room while she curled up on the bed and wept into her pillows.

Despite our history, my heart briefly ached for her, knowing how it felt to be taken by a husband one did not love. However, as I left the bedchamber, my mind quickly turned back to the most important issue at hand: the golden apple.

3: PARIS

Zeus turned the golden apple over in his hand, his thumb brushing over the shimmering skin as he sat on the throne. After several weeks of meditation, he had summoned all the Olympian goddesses to his presence with news of who would receive the apple. However, I imagine now that even for him it held some appeal, and he was finding it challenging to part from it.

Clumsy buffoon, I thought. *He will blemish it or worse.*

During those weeks, I had tried my best to find it but could never discover where Zeus had hidden the golden apple, despite how hard my nymphs and I had searched. Every day since the wedding, the goddesses of the court had confronted him, but he kept it hidden. In contrast, Eris had not stopped fomenting envy among us all, telling each one the apple was hers. My youngest daughter had not spared me from her tormenting words either, having approached me in my bedchamber one morning as I was weaving at my loom.

"Mother," she said, bowing respectfully and wearing a forlorn expression.

I looked at her. "What is it, Eris?"

She spoke in a quiet voice. "I wish to apologise for my behaviour at the wedding of King Peleus and Queen Thetis. It was impolite of me to ruin their wedding day."

I raised an eyebrow. "It was a little more than impolite, would you not agree? Your actions were rude and ruinous. They reflected badly on you and your family, including your father and me. In fact, it reflects poorly on the entire Olympian order, which is responsible for your elevated status in this universe."

She nodded, achieving a pink blush on her cheeks. "I am sorry, Mother."

"Sorry for your behaviour or for stealing from me?" I demanded. "That apple came from my garden. Do not deny it."

"I did not know it was your garden, Mother. I am sorry for that also." At least she had the grace to look embarrassed. "However, I did not think it would matter to you, as you already have one here in your bedchamber."

She gestured to the fruit bowl on the cabinet in the corner of the room, where Gaia's wedding gift to me all those centuries ago still stood, just as fresh as the day it had been plucked.

I pursed my lips. "That is hardly the point. Thievery is not to be pardoned lightly, but it is the royal couple of Phthia whom you harassed, casting the ugliest pall over their wedding celebrations."

She gasped slightly. "Mother, they did not invite me. Are you truly suggesting it was not unjust? Would you have acted any differently?"

I sighed. "I would not have behaved as you did."

She crossed her arms, scowling. "That is easy for you to claim."

"Is it?"

"You know well that you will never be left out of a Hellenic wedding."

"I should think not. It is my domain."

She closed her eyes. "Yes, that is precisely the point. You will never be excluded in that way. Just imagine if everyone was invited to something you were not. Can you even envisage how that would feel?"

I put down my spindle. "Yes, for I have experienced such things before."

"Oh, really? When?"

"When Demeter, Hestia and me were removed from ruling alongside our brothers. Exclusion does not get any worse than that," I snapped. "Yet I restrained my disappointment and hurt. I controlled my temper and did not make matters worse for anyone."

Eris's eyes widened, and her arms dropped to her sides. "I did not know that."

"You should have learned your family history better then," I remarked. "Apologise to the King of Phthia and his new queen. You cannot reverse time but you can try to heal the insult."

She huffed. "Fine."

Then her eyes grew wide and her voice sorrowful. "Do you forgive me, Mother? I stole from you and disrupted your work."

I was surprised. It seemed to be a genuine apology, something I had never heard from her before.

"I do," I heard myself say.

Eris beamed. "Truly? Thank you, Mother. I better get back. Father wants to ask me about the golden apple."

What? "What does he want to ask you?"

She shrugged. "I am not sure. Maybe he wishes to know who I think should have it."

I swallowed, my throat suddenly dry. "Who, in your opinion, would be so lucky?"

She pursed her lips thoughtfully. "I would say it is between you and Aphrodite. You are both, in my opinion, the finest goddesses in the universe."

Not quite the loyal answer I had been hoping for. "What makes you say so?"

She nodded, smiling. "Aphrodite is stunning, classically so, but she has the type of face multiplied by the hundreds by now. It is not special anymore. But you, Mother? You have a royal essence and serene divinity, which she ultimately lacks."

I smiled, grateful to hear it. "Thank you, Eris." Then I faltered. "Do you know who your father favours?"

She grinned. "Not yet. I suppose I shall soon find out. Farewell, Mother."

At first, the conversation had soothed my nerves, but when other goddesses at court informed me that Eris had said similar things to them, I knew she had also lied to me. However, it was now too late to restrain myself from the desire of wanting the golden apple. I was lost to temptation.

"Well?" Demeter snapped. "What is your decision?"

Zeus glanced up at his sister, remembering he was not alone but surrounded by the Olympian goddesses he had summoned to the throne room, all impatiently waiting, desperate to find out who was the most beautiful of them all. He sat up straight, holding up the bright fruit. He shook his head, seeming unsurprised.

"This is all it takes to occupy the female mind?" he murmured, more to himself than those in front of him.

Then he regarded us. "Well, it is not such an easy decision as you are all beautiful in your own way, like all aspects of nature."

His comment did nothing to assuage the minds and hearts of those who stood before him, a gathering of goddesses and nymphs who had now come to discuss the one thing that created such envy and insecurity between them: beauty.

All I could hope for at that moment, as I rubbed my fingers nervously, was that Zeus would choose his wife as the most beautiful goddess to avoid unwanted scrutiny on both of us.

Zeus pursed his lips slightly, glancing down at the apple in his palm.

Part of me dreaded he would take a bite out of it.

"However, I do not think I should be the one to decide. I would not want to risk dividing my household. So, I have decided to pass the decision on to someone else."

"To whom?" Aphrodite demanded, her voice strained in frustration.

"A mortal youth," Zeus announced.

I stared at him in disbelief.

Confused murmurings from the goddesses rose into alarmed protests.

"He is a prince of Ilion, a city once known as Troia, and, before that, Dardania. He is Paris, the son of King Priam. He is of my own line, has been educated excellently, and humbles himself by herding sheep in the nearby mountains, a prime example of goodness and sensibility. He has proven himself honest and honourable. He shall be the one to pass judgement."

I felt the annoyance rising within me. It was bad enough to have my beauty questioned — my status was publicly undermined. But to have the decision handed over to one with the same blood as Ganymede was contemptible.

"However, I cannot ask him to choose from all the divine women. So I shall select three candidates for him to choose between, those goddesses I think most deserve this prize. I shall give each of you a chance to recommend yourselves. Step forward if you think you are worthy of the golden apple."

Nearly every goddess stepped forward, including me, although some minor goddesses held back, possibly feeling unworthy. Hestia also refrained, not inclined to contest anything.

Zeus's eyes landed on someone towards the back of our group. "Even you, Athene?" he asked, sounding disappointed. "I would have thought you had better things to think about."

The deity of wisdom had stepped forward to be considered for the competition. They bowed their head. "I do, Father. Knowledge is beautiful too, and it should be represented in this competition," they explained proudly, declaring their position.

Aphrodite frowned. "My lord, Athene is not a goddess anymore. Is it right that they take part in this competition?"

Athene scowled. "As I said, the beauty of wisdom deserves to be represented."

Demeter shrugged. "Ares might say the same thing about war, but he is not here."

"Athene was born female," Zeus pointed out. "The vast majority of Hellas still worships them as a goddess, so they shall be allowed to participate."

Athene wore a triumphant smile, while Aphrodite glowered.

"Very well then." Zeus nodded. His eyes scanned those who had put themselves forward. "Carry on."

Like Athene, each goddess gave her reason for her worth, contending, in different ways, how her dominion over nature was the most precious and should be represented for its natural beauty and value in the world.

I could not believe that Zeus had not automatically selected me. However, I still stepped forward, saying, "As Queen of Olympos, the beauty of Heaven, marriage, motherhood, devotion, and duty to one's family is best represented by me."

Aphrodite defended herself with: "I am beauty. This apple is meant for me, my lord."

Afterwards, Zeus selected me as one of the candidates for Paris to choose from. However, my contestants were Aphrodite and Athene. Then he entrusted the Golden Apple to Hermes to deliver it to Paris.

We left for Ilion immediately.

As the sun fell over the side of Mount Ida, the night started to cover the eastern desert realm in dim light. Flying through the sky, I noticed the air began to get heavier with heat. The stars above my head were reflected like bright jewels in the sea beyond.

Prince Paris of Ilion was indeed shepherding on the hillside when we found him. He was a tall, handsome young man, with curly dark hair and brown eyes in a face deeply tanned from being outdoors. Of course, he fell to his knees when he caught sight of us approaching. Rising from his kneeling position, he gulped, faced with four deities and their challenge.

Hermes presented him with the golden apple. "Zeus has bestowed upon you, young prince, the honour of presenting one of these goddesses, Queen Hera, Aphrodite, or Athene, with the golden apple, a trophy which can only be awarded to the most beautiful goddess. It is your decision to make."

Paris glanced down at the apple, his eyes wide. Then he coolly turned to Hermes. "How can I judge them properly if I cannot see their full beauty?"

I blinked, both shocked and confused by the question. Was he asking what I thought he was asking? *What a demand to make of three goddesses! The impudence!*

Hermes glanced at us, unsure. "The goddesses will do whatever they deem necessary to win," he said. "From that, you must decide."

I glanced at the others. Athene's face was expressionless, impartial to the idea. On the other hand, Aphrodite was already naked, her dress pooling around her feet. Her golden locks fell by her sides, framing her curves with such precision that it would make even the most skilled artist blush.

My mouth dropped open.

Paris's eyes widened at her porcelain perfection.

Suddenly, Athene did the same. They gave me a sideways glance, as if to say, *It is the smartest way to win, my lady.*

I gazed at the princeling. There was nothing humble in him; he stood waiting, arrogantly staring at me with an obsessed hunger, imagining me naked.

Already aggrieved that I had to prove myself before some little upstart, I shivered, disgusted. However, I saw the apple in his hands with its skin the colour of the sun. And so, closing my eyes, I gathered my courage.

I slowly removed the brooch from my veil, which wrapped around my hair and neck. Then I unpinned my dress and let both fall to the ground. The cold wind of Mount Ida wrapped around my skin. Teeth chattering and skin shivering under the watchful gaze of Paris, I matched the competition. Yet I could not look at anyone else. I stared straight ahead, my heart racing.

Now unclothed, the contest began.

"Fine goddesses," Paris said. "Tell me why I should declare you the most beautiful."

"Paris," I began, looking away so as not to see his gaze slither over me. It did not work. I could still feel it. "Should you pick me, I shall make you a king. You have many older

27

brothers. Your chance of ruling Ilion by your own right and merit are none. Pick me, and these hurdles will be overcome. I shall not just make you King of Ilion, but with my blessing, you shall hold sway over the whole world."

I looked at him, staring back at me wide-eyed, no longer at my body but at my face, at the idea of all his wealth and power.

"Paris," Athene spoke up. Their voice was sharp and commanding. "Should you select me, I shall give you skill and wisdom. With these, you will have the knowledge to build an empire by your own hand, with greater fulfilment. Is that not better?"

"Paris," Aphrodite called to him sweetly, quickly getting his attention. "Should you choose me, I shall offer you myself."

Athene and I turned to her in shock.

Paris stared at her in astonishment.

"In human form," the goddess of love and beauty continued. "You shall lay claim to the mortal woman who is most like me in appearance, the most beautiful woman on Earth. How would it feel to have the goddess of beauty's earthly counterpart in your bed?"

All it took was for Paris to swallow his drool and nod lazily, ogling her bare body, for the golden apple, rightfully mine, to be Aphrodite's, for Helene of Sparta to be his, and for the world to fall into turmoil.

4: GERANA

Paris approached Aphrodite and knelt before her. He raised the golden apple in his palms. "My lady, I present the golden apple, which is rightly yours as the most beautiful goddess on Mount Olympos."

Aphrodite beamed. "I graciously accept this prize," she breathed, pleased with her victory. "Rise, Prince Paris of Ilion."

He did so, and she took the golden apple from him.

Gazing down at the apple held between her long delicate fingers, she turned it, the intense Phrygian sunlight making its golden skin look white.

I stared at the golden apple in her hand, anger coursing through my veins. I closed my eyes.

When I opened them and saw my naked body, my rage was replaced by humiliation. I had bared myself for this. *For him, the little wretch. For nothing.* I looked at Paris, taking in every detail of his face. I clenched my jaw. *What arrogance! He would forever regret this.* I would make sure of it.

I glanced up at the heavens to address the Moirai. I spoke to them in my mind, telling them that, from now on, for Paris and his kin, I would become both Fate and Fury in one. I would send him and the rest of his family to the depths; that much I swore to myself.

Aphrodite looked at Paris. "To you, sir, I promised the most beautiful woman in the world. I cannot provide her directly by hand, but I can tell you where she is, where you can find her and assure you that, as per my decree, she is yours by divine right."

He nodded, biting down on his lip, barely able to contain his excitement.

"Travel to Sparta, across the Aegean Sea. There you will find your prize: Queen Helene of Sparta, the wife of the king in Lakonia," Aphrodite instructed him. "But your recovery of her will not be easy. There are fierce folk in Sparta. Their women, too, are smart and steadfast, including the queen. You will need a clever stratagem to outwit them all."

Paris nodded, understanding his brief thoroughly.

I glared at Aphrodite, offended that she would part a wife from her lawful husband, a king from his queen, just to honour her promise to this scavenger. The idea appalled me.

As we all departed from Mount Ida, I trembled with rage. How could I return home so disgraced by both Aphrodite, who had stolen what was rightfully mine and undermined the sanctity of marriage, and Paris? He was not worth stripping bare for. What had the measly little mortal done to deserve it? Indignant, ashamed, and furious, I decided to stay in the east, a land of people who I did not know and who hardly knew me, until I managed to overcome my humiliation.

And so, I wandered through the skies above Phrygia and south through Kappadokia, travelling with no purpose other than to clear my mind. Still, my anguish did not subside with the passing days as I reflected on how quickly the recent events had unfolded.

In my meditation, I failed to notice the darkening clouds from the west — Zeus was probably wondering why I had not yet returned home. As a tempest grew, I lost my bearings and was blown over land and sea. I have no idea how long I was tossed about, but at the first lull in the winds, I landed, eager for rest and to judge how far I was from home.

When my feet touched the earth, it was daytime for the humans. Stepping over the meagre patches of grass covering the hard rock, the heat of the sun on my skin was unbearable. I began to sweat as I trekked. For a long while, I wondered if the trees would never end until finally, I came to a great mountain. Its peak rose to the clouds. At the base, out of caverns in the rocks, came sallow-skinned children, chatting and laughing loudly. The boys were carrying spears. When I saw an even smaller human walk out of one of the huts, I realised they were fully grown, tiny mortals, no taller than the shrubbery. Then from among them, out strolled a woman, dressed in a shawl, with bare feet. She wore a golden necklace and matching bracelets up her arms.

The glade fell silent. The others bowed and parted as she approached, leaving their menial chores. I watched from behind the barrier of trees as she stood before them, all the attention focused on her.

"They say the King of the Gods has prostituted his own wife, aunt and daughter for the pleasure of a mortal man. Made them harlots for a piece of fruit!"

A ripple of laughter swept through the group.

"There is more," she continued. "Apparently, a lowly prince of Ilion was promised the most beautiful woman in the world by the goddess of love and beauty."

Murmurs rippled through her audience.

"In return for a golden apple! In doing so, he put even the queen of their gods beneath her!" She laughed, her bosom heaving with mirth.

My face went hot, my fingers digging into the tree bark. How such a story had reached the ends of the earth so quickly, I did not know.

"Well, you are more beautiful than all of them combined, my queen," one declared.

"Your beauty outmatches any Queen of the Gods, too!" another cried.

I blinked in shock, taken aback.

The woman laughed, flattered. "Oh, I am grateful to you all, for the outside should reflect what is within. I even hear that the soul of the gods' queen is warped by murder and hysteria."

The crowd burst into laughter, their merriment echoing all around me.

Furious, I charged out towards them. Pushing some of them aside, I strode right up to their queen, towering over her, letting her tremble in fear before grabbing her tightly by the jaw and lifting her off the ground.

They all fell silent and dropped to their knees, realising they were in the presence of no mortal pretender.

"Your name," I ordered.

She stared up at me in silent terror.

This only made me angrier. The dishonour was too much to bear.

"Your name!" I repeated, yelling in her face and squeezing my grip on her jawline.

"Gerana!" she screeched.

"So, you think you are more beautiful than me, Gerana?"

"No, my lady!" she gasped. "I-I was just —"

"Boasting," I snapped. "A trait as ugly as any. Yet you make a good point. The outside should reflect what is within."

I dropped her to the ground, letting her fall into an undignified heap. Then, casting my hand over her, I placed a curse upon her.

The people gasped and cried out in astonishment and grief.

Getting shakily to her feet, Queen Gerana of the Pygmies batted her wings and flew away with a mind as inferior as her actions when human, now a crane. Her winged descendants would torment her people for years to come whenever they migrated for the year's colder months. Such was the punishment for impiety.

Being laughed at made me realise I had wasted too much time feeling hard done by: the longer I stayed away, the more I would have to salvage.

I suppose it would have been naive to think Aphrodite would have put her victory quietly away. She carried that golden apple everywhere, just in case one would not know who she was by her visage and countenance. On her return to Olympos, I heard that even Zeus had climbed down from his throne to embrace and kiss her, claiming he had known all along that she would win and that there had never been any real competition. He threw a party in her honour. Even in this, I guess I should never have expected his loyalty.

Throughout the world, the boasting of Gerana confirmed the effects of Paris's decision: Aphrodite was the most beautiful. There was nothing more to be said on the matter. After Zeus, she became the most popular and potent deity on Olympos, worshipped on Earth below. From now on, all men wanted her, and all women wanted to be her. And it was no different on Olympos: courtiers' gazes went from my husband to her to me when they entered the courtroom. The crowds couldn't get enough of her, as if just being near her might make them more beautiful too.

After returning home, and in my humiliation, I stayed away, distracting myself with routine chores. I wove clothes. I cleaned bedsheets. I tidied my bedchamber and the nursery, even though no children were in it nowadays, with Eris now a maiden. I emptied out the amphorae and refilled them. When I could not find anything else to do, I walked outside in the courtyard and out to the forest at the rear of the palace. I strolled under the twilight. I wept for my loss, my lack of beauty. I lamented that no matter how many times I tried to prove myself or win personal victories, they were consistently stolen from me. I was sick of it.

The hatred in my soul for Paris prevented me from sitting still. He deserved to be punished. That much I knew. I would see to it that he was. No longer could I bear to restrain the vengeance I sought. So, I gave in to it. This time, however, was different. Now, I had justice on my side. Aphrodite had endorsed breaking apart a married couple. This I could not allow. It was a direct subversion of my laws and dominion. For this, Aphrodite, Paris, and anyone else on their side would face my wrath. Nothing would make me change my mind on that score.

5: ATHENE

Athene had become a distant figure. They were still listened to and respected, yet no one knew what to expect or how to treat them. No one seemed to understand their decision. Now, somehow, by declaring to be neither a god nor goddess, they were considered less than either. Many times, Athene had come to me in distress, feeling friendless. So, we decided they would take up residence elsewhere in Heaven.

Unfortunately, I had not spoken to them in a long time due to their physical absence from court. So, it felt like I was going to meet a stranger when I sought Athene out. I left the Olympian palace and walked through the city, past the temples and other houses, until I reached the gates leading out into the forest. I found Athene's temple, a tall marble building, standing firm despite everything its deity was suffering.

Walking inside, the place was lit by torches. At the end of the temple was a gold and ivory statue of Athene from when they had been Athena, in full battle dress, with Nike, the goddess of victory, by their side. Mounted on the walls around the statues was weaponry of different sizes and shapes. Some I did not even recognise. Among them was the Minoan double-headed axe, which I greatly admired. Reaching up a hand, I wondered if it was even sharp.

"Do not touch that!" a sharp voice exclaimed. "It is possibly older than you or I."

I jumped and turned around to see Athene standing behind me.

They were dressed in a tunic and sandals, showing nearly their entire legs. Their hair had been recently shaved off. They had a golden sword in their hand, pointing down to the ground.

They bowed their head. "My lady, how may I be of service?"

I blinked, realising I had not thought about why I had come. I searched for a reason. "I wanted to know if you were all right?"

They raised an eyebrow. "After so long? No, you wanted to know if *you* were all right, which you are not."

I nodded. "When I was in the east, there was an earthly queen, Gerana of the Pygmies. She insulted my beauty, agreeing with Paris. I was offended, of course, but more alarmed that word had already reached the world's edge."

Athene chuckled. "My lady, you were hardly at the edge of the world. There is much more land beyond. After that, one reaches the Far Sea and yet more land beyond again. Trust me, thousands have never heard of you, Helene, Aphrodite, Paris, or even me."

"All who matter know of it. They know of my shame."

"They know of mine too."

"You do not seem concerned."

They shrugged. "I have studied behaviours in both the divine and the mortal. Most take pleasure in the pain of others, often unintentionally, because it can help them feel better about their own situations. As for being embarrassed, there is no logic in worrying about something one cannot control. As for public scrutiny, I can only say that people already think I am a freak."

"Do you regret giving in to Paris's demands?"

Athene shook their head. "It was a competition, one that I fear Aphrodite was destined to win. However, we all did what we deemed necessary. Those not prone to hypocrisy will see that, and they will not judge us for it."

I could not so readily agree. "It is important that I have a good reputation."

"With all due respect, my lady, your reputation has been tarnished for some time. The only thing which has saved you so far has been Zeus's support."

I scowled. "His what?"

They smiled sadly at me. "I know it seems an incredible notion. However, you are the one he chose as his wife. You may hate him, but he has never done away with you. It shows everyone else that he believes you are worthy of being queen. Of course, he is probably just protecting himself. If he admits that you are not a good queen, it will show that his decisions can be flawed. That would bring his authority into question. He may treat you abysmally in private, but he will defend your honour publicly."

"If you are trying to help me to feel better, you are not succeeding."

"I am trying to make you see that you will never be undermined seriously by anyone, least of all Paris. Zeus will keep you on the throne. Furthermore, everyone knows that the goddess of marriage and motherhood as the Queen of Heaven makes sense. Zeus's offspring, whom you have raised, are all useful members of the court. Lastly, you are terrifying. No one would dare make an enemy of you."

Even though it was not their intention, that did made me feel better. "Nevertheless, I cannot allow Paris's insult to go unpunished."

They raised an amused eyebrow. "I would expect nothing less of you. As it happens, King Menelaos of Sparta has joined forces with his brother, King Agamemnon of Mykenai. He has called all the fighting men of southern Hellas, known as the

Achaeans, to camp at Aulis, sail across the Aegean Sea, and lay siege to Ilion."

"Do you think they will win?"

"The Achaeans have many experienced leaders. The Trojans have high walls in their favour, the ones that we slaved to build, myself included. They will be incredibly challenging to breach. We made sure of that at the time. The war will waste time, gold, and lives if they do not break through those walls. However, they should prevail, if the Achaean priest Kalchas is correct. He has foretold the war's victory in their favour. However, only the Moirai know for certain."

"Whose side will you take?" I eyed them carefully.

"I have yet to decide who is worthy of my help, for whoever I support will have a significant chance of victory." Athene tilted their head at me. "You will support the Achaeans, I presume."

"Indeed. It concerns me that you hesitate to do the same, after suffering the same as me."

They shrugged. "I did not suffer anything other than defeat in a minor competition."

I urged myself to stay calm, for I wanted to convince them to side with me, but I could not hold back my disbelief. "Minor? It has led to war! Zeus employed a snake to judge that contest. Then he shamed us both. Aphrodite's victory means that beauty only exists in those who look like her. Our inaction will confirm our acceptance that her version of beauty is the only version there is. Now the world laughs at us. People will believe that appearance is more important than intelligence or loyalty. Do you have no pride?"

They raised their head, their grey eyes glared thunderously at me. It was the look of their father. "Of course I do. I simply did not think of it like that."

"Do not lie. You think of everything. You have been sitting here weighing the pros and cons of serving either side. How about you serve the respect you deserve, something you did not get from that Trojan rogue?"

They hesitated for a moment. Then they nodded. "Very well. You have my support."

I shook my head. "That is not enough. I want your allegiance. We must do this together, not just you coming to my aid when I flounder. We must be a team."

Athene slowly smiled. "Agreed, my queen. I should like to see how the mind wages war instead of weapons."

6: HELENE

At this point, southern Hellas had been inherited by two families, each ruling dominions known as Sparta and Mykenai, which lay southwest of Athens's growing settlement. Since its inception, Sparta has been a military power. Due to Lakonia's isolated settlement in the centre of the Peloponnesian landmass, it was forced to overtake neighbouring tribes — who became eternal slaves known as helots — to reach the sea and establish trade routes. However, such an empire would forever require oppressive force to hold it together. At such a time in humanity's history, such a power could only come from military prowess. The men were the fiercest and bravest in the Hellenic world, practically invincible, while the women were also strong and healthy. Girls were permitted to wrestle and play sports just like their male counterparts to ensure that, once they were wed, they would more likely give birth to healthy baby boys. Such sons could more effectively serve as soldiers for the state. So, it is little wonder that Helene's glowing natural beauty and grit were encouraged and enhanced by the culture she grew up in.

The royal house of Sparta was descended from Perseus, the noblest demigod of the Heroic Age, whose adventures include the slaying of Medusa the Gorgon. She had once been a mortal woman. However, after Poseidon raped her in Athena's temple, she was cursed by the goddess to have snakes for hair that would turn anyone who so much as glanced at her to stone. Perseus killed her by using the reflection of his shield to direct his sword and strike her down.

Afterwards, he rescued Andromeda, Princess of Aethiopia, from being sacrificed to a sea monster which Poseidon had sent after the queen had boasted she was more beautiful than any of the sea nymphs. I could imagine Queen Thetis of the Nereides running to Poseidon like the spoilt brat she was and complaining to him about it. At any rate, Perseus promised King Kepheus of Aethiopia that he would slay the monster if he could wed Andromeda, for he had fallen in love with her at first sight when flying overhead on his winged sandals, gifted to him by Hermes. He had gazed upon the naked Andromeda, screaming while chained to a rock, about to be eaten alive, and found this captivating. The king hastily agreed, and Perseus rescued Andromeda.

At their wedding, her uncle, Phineas, caused quite a stir, revealing that she had been betrothed to him initially. Perseus efficiently diffused the situation when he presented Phineas with the decapitated head of Medusa, which retained powers of transubstantiation, turning him to stone.

Having neatly established himself as a traditional hero, slaying monsters and saving the innocent, loving his wife and protecting their union from ill-wishers, Perseus whisked Andromeda away to Tiryns near Argos. Their daughter, Gorgophone, married one Oebalus, founded a settlement called Lakonia further south, took over the nearby lands, and created the Kingdom of Sparta. They had a son named Tyndareus, who would be the husband of Helene's mother. However, it is crucial to understand that Helene was not his daughter.

The most beautiful woman of her generation throughout the Hellenic world was a bastard to the King of Heaven, and exactly like Aphrodite to behold yet without her divine essence.

With golden hair, her captivating beauty inspired and hypnotised all who saw her.

One might wonder why I never turned my hand against her, being an illegitimate offshoot of my husband. Well, the truth is threefold. The first reason was that I did not want to. I did not wish to destroy something so beautiful. I suppose I, too, was smitten in some way. The second reason was that even if I did want to, for this was a woman who had abandoned her first husband and taken another, I knew it would be seen as another hunt for a bastard of Zeus, and I did not wish to add fuel to the bonfire that was my reputation, as Athene had pointed out. The third reason I never personally persecuted Helene of Sparta was that I never had the chance, for everyone else wanted a bit of her too.

At dinner one evening, long before the Judgement of Paris, Zeus had proudly announced the birth of a mortal daughter. He described how he had transformed himself into a swan on the Spartan coastline. However, an eagle flying overhead liked the look of his white feathers, and a hunt began. Instead of changing back into his godly form and blasting the eagle out of the sky with a lightning bolt, he fled to Lakonia, where he was given refuge by a woman who took pity on him, throwing stones and sticks at the eagle until it abandoned the chase and flew away. She then picked up Zeus, still a swan, and carried him to safety. This woman was, of course, Leda, the wife of King Tyndareus. After gaining her affection, Zeus mated with her, still as a swan, and by him she became pregnant once more.

Tyndareus must have been delighted, so far only siring daughters. I bet he was biting his nails behind his wife's birthing chamber door. He must have jumped up and down at the sounds of the ladies on the other side. Unable to bear the suspense, he burst through the door and looked down on the birthing bed to see a gigantic egg, covered in blood and placenta, lying before his wife's open legs. That is how my daughter Eileithyia, the goddess of childbirth, reported it to me. I winced at the mention of the egg. Having given birth to one myself — Typhon — I knew it was a far more painful type of birth.

Shock, and possibly horror, must have been quickly replaced by wonder when the egg began to crack. Jumping away in surprise at this sudden movement, Tyndareus gasped along with the midwives as the egg burst open, bits of shell flying everywhere. Looking into the remains, Tyndareus saw a set of triplets: Kastor and Pollux, twin boys who became known as the Dioscuri, and Helene, the most beautiful baby girl in the world.

As he gazed at his latest daughter, Tyndareus forgot his two sons for whom he had waited years and suffered four daughters. That did not matter now. Helene was what mattered. She was precious to her father, the favourite of his children. She had to be nurtured, protected, and polished. Furthermore, the remnants of the eggshell from which she had been born were bound together and suspended from the top of the Spartan acropolis for all to gaze at as they walked by.

Helene only became more beautiful as she grew older. Soon word of Tyndareus's youngest daughter began to spread throughout the kingdoms. Theseus, King of Athens, had started to regret his abandonment of Ariadne all those years ago. So, he devised, along with his close friend, Pirithous, how they would each gain a beautiful, divine, and royal wife.

And so, Theseus kidnapped Helene, leaving her with his mother, Aethra, in Athens until she was old enough to marry, for, at this time, Helene was not yet ready to bear children. I imagine Helene had not been robbed of her dignity, and Theseus most likely was saving her for their wedding night. Although, again, Theseus never struck me as the most patient or considerate man.

Meanwhile, Pirithous chose Persephone. He and Theseus descended to the Underworld to kidnap her. Haides was immediately wary of living souls passing through his realm. So, he set a trap for them, causing the rock they had sat on to grow into their rears, chaining them to their seats, and planning to let them wither away and die there. However, Theseus managed to escape, while Pirithous was left behind to die. He returned home to find Helene and Aethra stolen away from Athens, which had been sacked in his absence, and destroyed by the Dioscuri, who had come to rescue their sister and taken Aethra as their hostage. Due to the devastation, Theseus was suddenly very unpopular with his people, who decided that a monarchy did not suit them. And so, democracy was born. King Theseus fled to the island of Skyros. He sought shelter with King Lykomedes, who threw him off a cliff after Theseus requested that his lands there be returned to him so he could have a kingdom of his own once more.

A few years later, Helene was finally of age. King Tyndareus knew he would have to find her a husband. Little did he realise how besotted the rest of the world had become with this beautiful maiden living across the sea, protected by a tribe of fierce warriors ready to defend her honour at all costs. Suitors from all over the Hellenic world sailed to Sparta's shores in desperate hope for even a glance of the famous Helene, never mind her hand in marriage. Tyndareus was hesitant and uncertain. He feared, once he saw the assembly of kings and princes before him, that war would break out should any of them go home unsatisfied. Unable to give them all what they wanted, he turned to the most intelligent man in the room for aid: King Odysseus of Ithaka. The latter was already betrothed to Princess Penelope, a daughter of a more diminutive Spartan lord and Helene's cousin.

Odysseus advised Tyndareus to force the suitors to vow not to fight amongst each other, no matter the summit's outcome. Fortunately, the suitors agreed, and oaths were made that none would clash over the hand of Helene, and they would have to protect her marriage with their lives. Then they drew straws for her hand, leaving the decision to the gods. Prince Menelaos of Mykenai was successful, although he was not there in person, being represented by his older brother, Agamemnon, the King of Mykenai.

Helene was enthralled by Agamemnon's great build and strength of character. At first, she thought she would wed the man himself but was soon disappointed by her eldest sister Klytemnestra. The latter proudly stated that she would marry the King of Mykenai instead. Tyndareus saw the benefit of the two strong kingdoms marrying into one another twice, so the alliance between the north and south was strengthened with the weddings of Helene to Menelaos and that of Klytemnestra to Agamemnon.

Soon afterwards, Tyndareus stepped down from the throne of Sparta and lived in retirement with Leda. I imagine their relationship had become fraught after she gave birth to an egg and confessed to coitus with a swan. Tyndareus could not look at his wife in the same way after that.

Helene and Menelaos became King and Queen of Sparta. Unfortunately, Menelaos, although very much like his older brother in physique and skill, was nowhere near as intelligent, erudite, or confident. Due to his childhood in which his family had killed and eaten each other, he greatly mistrusted anyone who was not a close friend. He found it difficult to open up to his new wife. Despite many efforts on her part to get to know him, her attempts were in vain. Menelaos, although very much in love with her, could only love her from afar. He disappointed his wife, who grew tired of trying to love him. Soon, she no longer enjoyed his company. One must understand that Helene was a romantic sort, like Aphrodite herself. She sought fun, excitement, beauty, and, above all, a good time. Her husband was not much of any of that. So, she sought something different, something new, fresh, strange, and exciting — or someone, perhaps.

Fortunately for Helene, Paris came to Lakonia on a diplomatic mission with other princes from the Troad region of Phrygia, representing his father's city of Ilion, proposing to forge trading links. It is noteworthy that King Priam of Ilion had sired fifty sons. All of them enjoyed a nobleman's status at the Dardanaian court, yet only thirteen were borne by his wife, Queen Hekabe. When I think of her plight at her husband's disgraceful and lecherous behaviour, I almost count myself lucky with Zeus, as not even the King of Heaven had reached that many bastards that I was aware of. I suppose it could be said that Priam was not a king entirely devoted to the reign of his empire. On the other hand, he was considered the most successful King of Ilion so far. It was peacetime, and his kingdom was prosperous. I wondered how a busy king with a mortal lifespan of sixty or so years could find the time to raise fifty sons and still rule efficiently.

The Spartans also wondered about this, which went against Paris at the summit. King Menelaos was not keen on foreigners. He was very much like his people in that regard. Spartans were never the most welcoming or tolerant bunch, introducing strict citizenship and migration laws early in their civilisation. Menelaos himself was especially not keen on lazy foreigners like Priam. However, luck was on Paris's side, as he persuaded Menelaos that his father's trading routes further east were vastly advantageous to anyone who wanted to participate. So he was allowed to stay at the palace longer, which suited a man wondering how to abduct his host's wife.

I can imagine how fast his heart was beating when Paris finally laid eyes on the prize that was his by right, promised to him by a goddess. He considered himself to be her valid owner. Such a word can be faithfully used to describe the marriages of ancient Hellas, where women were not legal entities with rights to independence, equality or property. Instead, they were property themselves. However, I had also heard reports that Helene, bored in her marriage, was at the very least curious about these strangers from far lands and was flattered by the attentions of Paris, who made every effort to get close to her.

It would not have been easy for Paris to devise how to snatch the Queen of Sparta away. To seize her from her quarters would have been tantamount to suicide — he would have been caught by the guards and executed by the king. All houses, even those of Sparta, were divided into male and female quarters. Even if it had not been a palace with guards constantly at their vigil, Paris would have had to pass by the other male residents, thereby drawing attention to himself, before he even arrived at the women's quarters. Such a place was usually located either at the back of the house or the top floor, the farthest place possible from the front door, so if a woman ever tried to leave the house, she would be seen by all her male relatives while passing through. She could be promptly sent back to her rightful place. Helene would have spent most, if not all, of her time there.

Paris must have realised that he would have to heed Aphrodite's advice and think of a clever stratagem to outwit them all. Fortunately, he had at least won the reasonable opinion of his hosts. In fact, Menelaos decided to trust the foreigners to such an extent that he undertook an expedition to Krete, leaving Paris with Helene. Only later, when Iris came to him to tell him the news, did he learn that Helene had been taken from him. Perhaps the Spartan king's absence finally gave Paris the audacity to carry out his plan.

In the days before the Trojans were due to return to the east, merchants who had travelled with him had remained docked at the port, the last of their wares laid out. Queen Helene and her ladies ventured out to see what was on offer. Paris found her and invited her for a meal on his ship amid the crowds. She would have agreed, either out of politeness to her guest or out of a genuine desire to spend time with him. Either way, Paris could not have kidnapped her among a crowd of Spartans. Helene must have gone willingly on board that ship. Whatever she may have thought or intended regarding Paris, she never left. And so, the circumstances of her remaining on board are unknown. However, rumours spread that Paris talked her into coming with him, that she readily stayed of her own free will, and that she lay with him that night. Others claimed these were lies. Why would a queen give up her luxury and security for a stranger's promises? Maybe Paris threw her into a cabin and locked the door.

Perhaps Helene did know Paris well somehow. Maybe they had a genuine, caring relationship. Maybe her life at home was hellish enough, despite being a queen, to agree to such an uncertain future, enough to leave her culture behind, risk raging seas, and abandon her children. Then again, perhaps Paris came to Sparta to take what the gods had said was rightfully his in whatever way he could, damning the consequences and ignoring whether or not Helene truly wanted him. As far as he would have seen it, the gods were on his side, even me, and he would not be punished by any divine hand for his actions.

I never said he was intelligent.

Whatever happened, a few hours later, Paris left the ship while Helene was still on board. He returned to the palace to find the queen's ladies distraught at their loss of her, with the guards informed of the missing queen. Paris and the Trojans took the opportunity of the chaos to leave early, saying they did not wish to trouble or intrude upon the poor Spartans any longer amid such a crisis. They left that very evening, carrying the beautiful Helene to Ilion. King Menelaos then returned to Sparta in haste, only to find the reports to be true. Perhaps this is what truly cemented the everlasting Spartan suspicion of foreigners.

At least, that is how I imagine the rapture of Helene happening. No one knows for sure. There are many theories, and this is just mine.

What is certain is that upon arrival at Ilion, Helene was welcomed by the Trojans as the wife of Prince Paris. She was introduced to the royal family and presented before King Priam. The mere sight of her soothed any suspicion about her. Even in the east, she was still the most beautiful of women. The public adored her. Everyone was just as obsessed with her as those on Hellas.

I am told a wedding ceremony was held, a very grand affair. Since it took place outside the Hellenic world, I had no divine right to supervise it. Helene now belonged to the Trojans. If they had a deity of marriage, it was that god's responsibility to preside over the affair, not mine. I understand she went on to bear several children for Paris during her time at Ilion.

However, as far as I am concerned, it did not matter that Paris and Helene were wed in Ilion. It did not matter that everyone in that city believed she was his wife and that she gave him children. The whole effort to make her the legitimate spouse of Paris was illegal under Olympian law since she already had a husband who had not formally divorced her.

At the same time, men could keep concubines, have an affair with another woman as long as she was not married, seek out prostitutes, and even practise polygamy in some Hellenic city-states. I am not saying the practice of monogamy is correct or just. Still, it was the law, and I concede that it was entirely hypocritical. A woman did not marry a man like a man married a woman. In effect, for a man, his wedding day was when he bought a pretty creature which could satisfy his lust, do his cooking and laundry, and multiply his family. She might hope for compassion and consideration but had no right to it and would have been foolish to aspire to love. She made his life easier by serving him and was ultimately a means to an end.

So for Menelaos, not only had his beautiful wife been kidnapped, but his property had been stolen, right from under his nose. Menelaos and all the Achaeans were entirely in agreement that this marriage to Paris did not make her a Princess of Ilion — she was just a mistress to one of its many princes and a traitor to her faithful husband. She had promised Menelaos on her wedding day to be loyal to him. He had made the same promise to her, and so far, it seemed he had kept it. He may not have been a perfect husband, but he had not been disloyal. Why would he desire another woman when he already had the most beautiful one? He had been personally and publicly humiliated. He had no option but to bring her back.

He would have had no standing in his kingdom or amongst his peers if he didn't. Otherwise, what would stop anyone else from taking what they wanted?

The retrieval of the Queen of Sparta did not go well. At first, the Achaeans tried to recover Helene of Sparta diplomatically, going with Odysseus on a mission to the Trojan city, but they were rebuffed. Then Menelaos called on the suitors of Helene to honour their pledge to Tyndareus, to protect his marriage, to gather their forces and set sail to bring her back. Unfortunately, after the Achaean forces set sail, they lost their way and were scattered by the winds. It was frustrating to see but recalling Athene's words, all we could do was watch on and wait for them to regroup. That was no mean feat. It took eight years for them to gather once more at Aulis.

When they finally did, it was an incredible sight of more than one thousand ships and at least one hundred thousand men, ready to fight to take Helene home. *At last*, I thought, *an army large enough to humble Paris*. Only this time, the wind did not blow. Not a puff! They waited and waited, eager and frustrated.

Then the blame game started with word that Agamemnon had hunted a deer sacred to Artemis, and she was preventing the wind from blowing. The soothsayer, Kalchas, instructed Agamemnon to sacrifice his eldest daughter Iphigenia to appease the goddess so they could proceed to Ilion. Agamemnon, heart tormented with grief and guilt, summoned Iphigenia with his wife Klytemnestra to Aulis under the pretence that a marriage had been arranged between his daughter and the hero Achilleus. While Klytemnestra soon realised the trick and confronted her husband, Iphigenia was swayed by the actual cause of Agamemnon's actions and, for the pride of Mykenai and the war effort, willingly walked to the altar to have her throat slit. The wind picked up, as did the mood in the ranks, feeling assured of victory.

At first, I was furious with Artemis that she would insist on such a high price. However, it had the opposite effect if she had wanted to weaken the Achaeans; for now, Agamemnon's resolve only grew: now, not only were they fighting for Helene but for the memory of Iphigenia. It showed how ruthless this war would become.

Alas, Athene was right. The walls proved too much: too high, too thick, too strong. Menelaos and his allies laid siege for nine years, but the Trojan court would still not concede to give Helene back. Nor, it seems, did Helene make any effort to leave, or at least there are no reports of her attempts to return home to her true husband. Even after the Achaeans had finally crossed the sea, camped on the Trojan shores, and were there night after night, there is no record by any sleepless nightwatchman of the most beautiful woman in the world sneaking up to Menelaos's tent to make peace with him under cover of darkness.

Yes, I believed that Menelaos was fully justified in waging war on that city which held his wife apart from him and, as the goddess of marriage, I felt it was my duty to help him recover her and bring her back home to Sparta, her people, and her children.

7: PRIAPOS

During those first nine years that the Achaeans were at Ilion, I waged my own war on Olympos against Aphrodite, leaving Paris's fate in the hands of Menelaos. I knew I just had to wait for her to want something I could destroy, ruin, or sabotage.

I knew the Moirai were on my side when Aphrodite became pregnant with Dionysos's child, with whom she had an affair. The only hindrance to my plan was getting close enough to Aphrodite for everything to unfold. Locked away in Ares's quarters, she isolated herself in the final days of her preparation for giving birth. Time was running out, so I approached the door to her bedchamber just as a nymph emerged from the other side.

She stopped when she saw me and curtseyed. "My lady Hera, may I help you?"

"Yes, you can let me through."

The nymph blushed and stammered, "Forgive me, my queen, but the Lady Aphrodite is resting within. She is in a very delicate condition at the moment. She is not receiving visitors."

I huffed and raised an eyebrow. "She shall receive the only one who can help her during this time, do you not agree?"

Realisation dawned on her face. "Yes, of course, my lady."

"Run along, then," I instructed.

She obeyed, bobbing another curtsey and hurrying away.

I opened the door and walked into the darkened room, the curtains drawn over the large windows, and only a couple of torches lit on the walls. I closed the door behind me and engulfed myself in the shadows. I gave myself a moment for my eyes to adjust. Then I heard Aphrodite sound asleep in her bed, snoring softly.

Lying on her side, her golden hair streamed out on the pillow behind her.

I approached her bedside. Sitting beside her, I gently touched her swollen stomach and sensed the life within. It was an offshoot of love and wine, drunken passions, not an intended child but not an unwelcome one. *Well, at least for now.*

Aphrodite stirred slightly at my touch but did not seem to wake fully from her slumber.

I swallowed hard, realising I would have to quietly whisper the words so she would not hear me. All the while, staring at Aphrodite's peaceful face, her breath escaping her lips, her brows relaxed, and her body still, I undid the brooch at her shoulder and let her dress fall open, revealing her swollen belly. Opening a vial I had brought, I poured the potion — no more than a fingertip — onto my hand. I rubbed it onto her belly, pressing gently to her skin.

I chanted the lyrics to a self-made poem, an enchantment I had been festering in the depths of my soul for a long while now: "A child of beauty but shall inherit none. A child of love but shall receive none. A child of fertility but shall sire none." Then, removing my hand from her, I let the curse take hold, departing the bedchamber as quickly as I could, her mild snoring now turning to whimpers behind me as I fled, feeling triumphant in my revenge.

Over the last days of her pregnancy, rumours flew around the court as to the changed condition of the goddess of love, how she was feeling persistent pain in her womb, headaches, and chest pains, how wretched she looked, and how she feared for her baby's health, for she sensed that something was amiss.

Ares's moods grew sour. He picked fights with the physicians over his paramour's wellbeing. No solution was good enough unless the pain completely subsided, which it did not. He even tried to convince Aphrodite to do away with all other doctors and instead seek my counsel on improving matters. Still, the goddess flatly refused to consider such a proposal; she did not trust me with the welfare of her child or herself.

After several more days and nights, word finally reached me that the baby had been born in the night, news delivered by a rather frazzled-looking Eileithyia.

I stared at her, taking in her dishevelled state. "What is the matter?"

She looked nervous. "I wonder if I did something wrong, Mother."

"Why would you think that?"

"You better see for yourself. I must tell the others." She curtseyed and rushed away.

I got up, hurried to my eldest son's quarters, and let myself inside. When I entered the chambers, Ares wore an expression as sinister as the grave, clenching a goblet of wine in his hand.

"Do not go into the bedchamber, Mother," he said. "Just stay away."

"What has happened?"

He shook his head. "In truth, Aphrodite has birthed a monster. Dionysos is distraught."

Fighting the urge to grin, I wore a forlorn expression. "How terrible."

He huffed and ran a hand through his hair. "I told her to speak to you before she gave birth. She did not listen."

"It is not your fault, my dear. There is no fault here. Although, I fear Aphrodite does not love me as she once did."

At that moment, I saw the opportunity to gain his support as the god of war should matters become messy with her. It would be tricky to get him to keep his word, but having it, nonetheless, could be helpful.

I placed a gentle hand on his. "Should Aphrodite and me ever become enemies, my dear boy, can I rely on you? It may not be pleasant to hear, but you should know that my love for you, as your mother, will always run deep and true, no matter what."

He hesitated, frowning at me. "I know that and will always be loyal to you, but why would you ever think you and Aphrodite would be enemies?"

I shrugged. "She is the goddess of love. She feels her emotions passionately and sometimes, if I may be so bold, does away with rationality. I have a terrible feeling that one day she will act in such a way as to force you to choose between us. I hope you understand that I would never do such a thing to divide your loyalties."

He pursed his lips. "I know, Mother, but I hardly think it will come to that."

I nodded, smiling. Deep down, I was concerned that Ares, although the god of war, was not too sharp at sensing when it was on the horizon.

"Let me see the child now," I told him.

Ares nodded and led me to a door I had never seen past before.

"You are not taking me to Aphrodite?"

"No, she will not see anyone, not even the baby." He opened the door. "In there."

I stepped into a small candlelit room with a cradle inside. The crying was the first thing I heard; that awful, ugly wailing. Approaching, I saw a grotesque sight, with an enormous member, constantly erect, amid balled, angry fists waving in the air and tiny kicking feet.

The baby was so hideous and misshapen that the throne room erupted in horror when he was presented to the royal court. Only when everyone had overcome their fright and dismay were the Moirai summoned. They named him Priapos, the god of fertility and growth, the personified phallus.

Aphrodite was ashamed that something so ugly had come from her, having swanned about the court, telling everyone how perfect she was. Once she had the energy to leave her bed, she abandoned the baby on a hill, leaving it kicking and screaming, where she intended it to perish. Dionysos did not object. He mourned his son, but more so that he had been born.

The door to my bedchamber flew open.

I turned to see Aphrodite, face red and puffy from crying, her hair dishevelled, looking at me like she wanted to carve me in two.

"What is the matter?" I asked, taken aback.

Her whole demeanour was of pent-up anger, ready to burst. "Only two beings in the universe can manipulate a pregnancy. You," she snarled, baring her teeth, "and your daughter, Eileithyia. Yet only one of you has something against me."

"I do not know what you are implying, Aphrodite."

"Stop lying to me!" she shouted.

I decided to stand firm. "How can you possibly know a lie from the truth?"

She stepped toward me. "I cannot, yet I know *you*. I know exactly who you are, Hera. I know that there is no one else, not one in the world, who could have done that to my son, to me, and who had every reason to do it."

I raised an eyebrow. "Do you have proof?"

She stared at me for a moment and then heaved a heavy sigh. "No."

"Then you cannot know it was me."

"You did it. I know you did."

"Then I shall ask once again. Where is your proof?"

"You do not deny it!"

"I shall not honour your accusation with an answer."

"Hera, do not expect me to behave honourably when you have not. You cursed my son. I do not need proof to carry out my own justice."

I drew myself up to my full height. "Do what you must. I shall do the same. Yet remember that no matter what you do, you can never change the facts: you, supposedly the most beautiful creature in the cosmos, gave birth to the ugliest creature to roam it. That is something that you can never take back. So, carry out your justice, for all the good it will do you and your son."

We glared at each other, full of fury and spite, until one of us broke.

Relief washed over me when it was her. She was emotional. She was fragile. So, she left first, and lost.

Did I regret what I did to Priapos? At this stage, maybe a little. No child deserved to be so disfigured and rejected. I knew that deep down. But he was nothing more than a pawn at this point, to wound Aphrodite. It was not until later, when others got hurt, that I began to regret creating him.

Nine years later, Priapos returned to court, alive and well, on the verge of manhood, to the surprise of all. He presented himself before Zeus and his family, saying he had been raised by shepherds who had discovered that his manhood helped plants grow. He was not as ugly as he had been when he was born. He had inherited his father's shaggy hair and impish smile. But he was inclined to fall forwards, so he had to walk with a cane to balance himself.

It was an awkward reunion, to say the least. No one knew how to react, but after his initial surprise, Dionysos embraced his son fondly. Aphrodite brought herself to give him a kiss on the cheek but no more.

Priapos and his father became very close. Dionysos had always longed to have a father figure, so he put great effort into Priapos's education on Olympos. Unfortunately, much like both his parents, Priapos had little self-control or restraint. On the one hand, he was good-natured and did not wish harm upon anyone, while on the other, there was a wild, daring streak in him. Once, Dionysos enchanted a particular donkey, whom he was fond of, to be able to speak. After Priapos and the donkey began to talk, they contested to see who had the longest phallus. When Priapos won, he killed the donkey. In grief, Dionysos placed the donkey among the stars.

Despite this, Dionysos continued to have faith in his son and welcomed him to all his parties. At one in particular, attended by all the gods and held in the ballroom, he learned the true nature of his son. Like most, it was dark, loud, drunken, and crazed. This time, he even had animals in the fray, including donkeys. As the crowd became raucous, one of the donkeys brayed loudly — so loud it drowned out the drums — and brought the music to a halt and everyone's attention to a shocking sight.

When I saw it, I stopped dancing and dived forward. I ripped Priapos off the couch, pushing him to the floor. I leaned down and checked my sister Hestia's breath as she lay asleep on the couch. Her skirts had been raised to her hips, so I pulled them down again.

Then I turned and shouted down on Priapos: "You miserable monster! How dare you!"

Dionysos surged forward, pushing past his guests. He hauled Priapos to his feet.

"Hera, what are you doing?" Dionysos shouted.

I gestured to Hestia. "Did you not see what he was about to do to her? He was going to defile her as she slept!"

Hestia started to wake at the raised voices.

Dionysos's face paled. He glanced at Priapos, shocked. "Is this true?"

It took Priapos a moment to realise that everyone was staring at him. He let out a nervous chuckle. "Of course not, Father."

"Cease your lies," I spat. "If not for that donkey, her honour would have been lost."

Hestia looked horrified, sitting up, not believing what she was hearing.

"Do you think it is easy for me?" Priapos protested, his face contorting with frustration and anger. "To walk around like this every day and never have relief? Just because I am disfigured —"

"Silence!" I roared, unwilling to accept his excuses. "My own son Hephaistos suffers physical defects. He, too, committed similar wrongs. However, he accepted them, learnt from them, and so was forgiven for them."

Then Zeus stepped forward from the crowd of bodies. His silver eyes were dark. "The queen is right. Hestia has taken a vow of maidenhood which everyone has always been able to respect. If Priapos cannot do the same, he must leave the court."

Dionysos gulped. "My lord, allow my son the chance to learn from this mistake. He did not succeed."

Zeus hesitated and then nodded. "Very well. I have shown such forgiveness before to others."

Relieved, Dionysos spoke to his son. "Go. I shall speak to you in the morning."

Priapos turned to leave.

I turned to Zeus. "What if he does not learn self-control? You heard him. He finds it difficult."

Zeus's face darkened. "Are you questioning my judgement, wife?"

"No, my lord. I question the reliability of Priapos's ability to learn self-control and respect for those goddesses who have taken an oath of virginity."

My husband sighed and rubbed his forehead. "All right, Hera. You have made your point."

He turned to Priapos. "Leave now. If you ever come back, that manhood you are so proud of will be struck from your body. Then you shall truly have nothing by which to prove yourself."

Priapos's face paled. He glanced between Zeus, his father, and me before fleeing the room and running down the mountainside back to wherever he had come from.

Hestia was not Priapos's first victim nor his last. He would forever chase those who did not want him. Once, he pursued a nymph called Lotis, who could not evade him no matter how hard she tried. Out of pity, the gods transformed her into a plant, the lotus flower. Notorious, Priapos left Hellas for distant shores.

Perhaps I scolded the godling so heatedly because of the brewing guilt within my own soul, seeking to distance myself from him as much as possible. But, after my rage eventually settled, I was greatly conflicted. I had created Priapos, but was I truly responsible for his actions? There was no excuse in my eyes for that kind of behaviour, none at all. And yet, perhaps, if he had been born differently, without my interference, he would have been different. It was a question for the Moirai, and I was too focused on my revenge against Aphrodite and Paris to face the matter myself.

8: MANIA

The battleground of the Trojans and Achaeans was a wasteland of blood, piled high with destroyed armour and shattered weaponry, severed body parts and broken spirits. The air reeked with the stench of decay and was filled with smoke, sand, and dust. Yet the sky above was still so blue, untouched by the Earthly chaos. Along the white shoreline was the large Achaean camp on one side of the battleground and the towering stone walls of Ilion on the other. Both were baking under the sun — Helios was not making this easy for either side.

I felt the rays, the sweltering heat, on my face. I was glad not to be a deity of war traipsing around all day in a heavy breastplate under this weather.

"Hera?" Athene's voice said from beside me.

I turned to them, and in doing so, I glowered at the massive walls of Ilion behind in the distance and framed by the mountains beyond. Hot rage flickered within me to think of Paris still there, ensconced within the safety built by the hard labour of my family.

"Let us begin," I said, not taking my eyes off Ilion.

Shrouded under a spell of invisibility, Athene and I made our way to the Achaean camp, passing through the gates and walking amongst the warriors. Most were lowly soldiers, there to follow and not to lead. We passed by large makeshift tents, temporary altars and wooden huts. Beyond, closer to the sea, were large pyres of burning bodies. We halted amidst the throng as we arrived outside the tent of Achilleus, with a group of heavily armoured men going inside.

I forsook my invisibility to appear before Achilleus in his tent.

He was an enormous man, although not of the might of Herakles. Tall, lean and golden-headed, he was bronzed from his days in the sun. He had a determined square-set jaw and startling turquoise eyes, the same as his mother, Thetis. They looked at me with terror, as he realised who I was.

He fell on one knee. "Queen Hera, this is the highest honour."

I glanced around at the scattered clothes, the upturned baskets, the muddy, bloody breastplate lying in the corner, including the cloak I had given as a wedding present to Thetis, that she might give it to her first son, and the remnants of a fire from the night before, a messy hearth in the centre of the ground. "Arise."

He got to his feet, keeping his eyes lowered in respect.

"Why is it that a soldier, especially one such as you, intends to hide here, where it is safe and warm?" I tilted my head at him.

He swallowed. "My lady, the camp is riddled with plague. Lord Apollo shoots down our men, sending them to Haides below before they can ever meet the Trojans on the plains outside. Those who have survived this far only venture out of doors when called upon by a commander. Those who make it to the battleground are already terrified for their lives. It is impossible to boost morale when we cannot even feel safe inside our own camp."

I frowned. "Why has Apollo enacted this reign of terror upon the Achaeans?"

"He fights for the Trojans," Achilleus stated. "King Agamemnon took the daughter of a Trojan priest of Apollo for his war prize. Her name is Chryseis. Many days ago, her father begged for his daughter to be returned to him, yet Agamemnon refused. And so, Apollo is seeking revenge on the priests' behalf, and now we suffer for Agamemnon's selfishness. It is not the first time either. He retains much of what is taken in sieges and battles for himself, despite not having set foot on the battlefield since landing on these strange shores. Apollo defends the family of his priest."

So Apollo was fighting for the Trojans. That irked me. Athena and I would need more allies if we were to win this war.

"Call a council of all the leaders of the various factions in the camp. Demand Agamemnon protect his men by returning the Trojan wench," I instructed him.

A slight fear entered Achilleus's turquoise eyes.

"My lady," he said, sounding hesitant.

I raised an eyebrow at him. "Would you disobey me, Lord Achilleus? Surely you have heard tales about those who wrong me." I stepped forward. "Your nerves will not do, not here, not with me. I expect to see the fierce and fearless warrior I was told was born to Peleus. You may not be my son, but I nursed your mother at my breast. It is the only reason I do not have you smitten into the earth below — I am within you too. Do not disappoint me."

He nodded and clenched his jaw. "I will do as you command, my queen."

Satisfied, I departed the tent. Finding Athene waiting for me outside, we headed towards the home of Agamemnon.

At the great round table in the council hall of Agamemnon's abode, Achilleus took up a seat next to Odysseus. The King of Ithaka was shorter, with nearly black hair and a neat beard. His dark brown eyes surveyed the room. He wore a slight smirk on his lips, whereas Achilleus tended to scowl.

A few more men took their places at the table. There was Achilleus's cousin, Patroklos. Further down the table was the old King Nestor of Pylos; King Idomeneus of Krete; the healer, Machaon; Kalchas, the soothsayer; and the famous veteran warrior, Phoenix. Next to him was Aias, commander of the Lokrians, also known as Great Aias because his son, Aias the Younger, had also come with him to Ilion. In time, poor Aias would suffer a fate almost worse than death. He would eventually lose his mind on the plains of Ilion and slay the Achaean reserves of sheep in his madness. Then, realising his deeds and unable to bear the humiliation of how low he had fallen, he would take his own life.

Finally, the men who needed no introduction, the instigators of this expedition, took their places: King Menelaos of Sparta, the husband of the kidnapped Helene, and King Agamemnon of Mykenai, the two sons of Atreus and the most influential lords on the Hellenic mainland, with Agamemnon, the older sibling, being the most powerful man in the world. It was clear they were brothers. Both were large, their bulk once strong muscle now turning to fat. They were the most finely dressed men in the room, with shining brass armour and thick cloaks on their backs; both wore the same pomposity and vanity in their expressions. Interestingly, Menelaos was more ostentatious in his dress. Still, it was Agamemnon, the taller, who held himself in such a way that it was inarguable that he was the chieftain in charge.

After their arrival, the meeting began.

Athene and I stood invisible in the corner of the room, watching the proceedings unfold.

The chieftains argued with each other on what their subsequent actions should be. It immediately became apparent that there was already a rift in their ranks, with Achilleus leading the opposition against Agamemnon.

"I have learned that Apollo is fighting against us," I whispered to Athene. "So, this begs the question: who is on our side?"

They sighed in thought. "Poseidon, Hephaistos, and Achilleus's mother, Thetis."

I clenched my jaw at the names but tried not to huff in disapproval. In wartime, one could only take what one got. Resources ran low, as did loyalty. Perhaps they would redeem themselves yet.

"Why Poseidon?" I asked. "He has no loyalty to the Achaeans, surely? I understand that Hephaistos shall fight for me, but why Poseidon?"

Athene shrugged. "I believe it has something to do with his previous experiences here. He once sent a sea monster to Ilion during the reign of King Laomedon as punishment for not paying him for his toils at the walls."

"Was this when Zeus sent them into slavery?"

Athene shook their head. "No, afterwards. Apollo and Poseidon wanted to test whether or not Laomedon was a good king. So they took on more work themselves. Both were insulted when they weren't paid. Apollo sent a plague, Poseidon a sea monster."

I frowned. "What happened to the sea monster?"

Athene pursed their lips in thought. "I believe Herakles killed it. It sounds like something he would do."

I sighed. "Well, not to worry. Ares gave me his promise that he would fight for me should the day ever come when I was at war with Aphrodite."

"So why has he reportedly been fighting at Aphrodite's side against the Trojans?"

My heart fell at the betrayal, but I tried not to take it too heavily, for I knew that mother's only have so much sway compared to lovers. However, with Ares at their helm, our enemies were bound to prevail. Paris would live on with personal victory and national pride, Aphrodite's gift by his side.

Our conversation was interrupted when the King of Mykenai submitted to the will of his chieftains, saying he would return Chryseis to her father if he received Achilleus's war captive Briseis in recompense.

Achilleus jumped to his feet and unsheathed his sword, pointing it in Agamemnon's direction. "You will not take her!"

The other warriors lunged forward to stop him. Shouts raised into the air, and other weapons were drawn.

Huffing in exasperation, I turned to Athene. "Stop this nonsense before that fool destroys this entire expedition."

They frowned at me. "Why can you not do it?"

"A word from the wise is what is needed now. Do me this favour."

Rolling their eyes, Athene used their divine power to freeze every man in the room in their place, except for Achilleus. They moved between the statues towards him and gave him the check he needed that he was about to create an irreversible disaster.

After the meeting was ended, I took the opportunity to explore the camp, invisible to the eyes of many. The sights, sounds, and smells were nothing to enjoy. The potent stench of excrement, sweat, and blood filled the air. Flies buzzed in the sweltering heat, flitting from the detritus of human waste to the rotting corpses of animals tracked down and hunted for food. The dogs were vicious and had to be held back from killing each other. Bannermen from different factions picked fights with each other. There was not one avenue or step I took where someone was not drunk, pissing or brawling. Discipline in the camp was nowhere to be seen.

On this score, Achilleus had been right. After long battles, sieging and failing, their supplies were running low, as was morale. On top of this, they faced a plague. The leaders were clinging to power, keeping all the gold for themselves. The only reward these men had was at night when they went to their war slaves and forced them into their beds.

I peered briefly into the compound where the captured women were kept: Briseis, Chryseis, Tekmessa, Kassandra, and so on. Looking at them, dressed in rags with thin veils around their faces, starved, stinking, covered in sweat and grime, it was impossible to tell which was which. Some had fair hair, some dark. Some were crouched in the corner, scavenging dead flies and spiders for food. Others were up on their feet, telling stories and trying to keep the morale high.

I saw no spirit among them and certainly no hope. It was a sorry sight, and my heart felt heavy for them. Yet, as I turned away, I knew that if it had been the other way around, and the Trojans were besieging Athens in Mykenai or Lakonia in Sparta, the situation would be the same with famine, plague, bloodshed, slavery, rape, torture — all the inhumanity imaginable. If the women and children were not killed, they would be reduced to slaves, their past lives obliterated. War was all the same in the end.

However, none of that changed my mind as I stared up at the high walls of Ilion. I remained determined that the wastrel Paris would be brought low — in shame or slavery or to Haides, preferably the latter.

With that in mind, I turned my attention back to the Achaeans. They had to raze the city to the ground and return Helene to her husband. Looking around the depraved campsite and the cowardly soldiers hiding in their tents, annoyance stirred in my breast.

I removed my shroud of invisibility so I could be seen, rose to my full imperial size and roared as loudly as possible for all to hear: "Good Achaeans! I speak to you as Hera, the lady on Mount Olympos, wife of Zeus."

Heads looked my way. People halted in their course. Faces emerged from the tents, and when the eyes of the army and their auxiliaries fixed upon the Queen of Heaven, many were frozen in fear and wonder. Then, of course, they fell to their knees. The heroes and kings of Hellas were among them, having just left the council meeting, unsure of what was happening.

"What are you doing?" Athene hissed. "We are supposed to keep a low profile, Hera."

I ignored them and continued, standing before the large crowd of soldiers: "Beyond this camp, there are thousands upon thousands of men, good soldiers, great warriors, led by a foreign mogul with an eastern empire, who have no qualms in stealing your women and tricking you. They wish to kill you all, whether in your sleep or in the fray of battle. You know this."

I cast an angry eye upon them all. "Yet you are letting them! You hide here in your tents, starving, wounded, sickly, wondering if the Moirai even know you exist. Well, I have come here to tell you that they do.

"While you may believe your fate is set, there are those for whom the Moirai will intervene and those they will let determine their own course through life towards death.

"You should look upon the world around you, the sky above you from where you came, the earth below you where you will undoubtedly end, and wonder whether that person might be you. I cannot say whether you are or not; it is not my decision.

It is yours. Yesterday. Today. Tomorrow. Ten years, a hundred years from now. It does not matter what day it is or where we are when you can rise from your bed every morning and choose to turn your dreams into reality. You can choose to be that person who alone decides when they will meet their end. It is possible. It can happen here and now.

"Are you truly going to let those barbarians out there determine your fate? Are you going to see your wives and children once more before you rest for eternity? Or are you going to see your homeland again, the wide green fields and forests of Hellas, instead of these barren deserts? Or are you going to perish here at the will of marauders and thieves?"

I let my words hang in the air. As I looked around, the fear and shock in the eyes of the Achaeans had been replaced by a determination to achieve what they set out to do, then to return home or die trying. I knew, at the very least, I had done my part.

I caught Athene's frown of disapproval as I ended my speech. I heard their mutterings of how my anger against Paris would be remembered. "You must not let your emotions cloud your judgement."

I ignored them. I would not be persuaded to stand on the sidelines. The fury, the mania, in my heart was too much to quell.

9: THETIS

Agamemnon was merciless in his greed. Once he had put Chryseis on a ship bound for her father, he ordered guards to move Briseis from Achilleus's tent and bring her to his. When Achilleus found her gone, he withdrew his troops, bolted down to the seashore, and complained to his mother about it.

"What did he say to her?" I asked Athene from my seat at the table.

We were in my tent within the Achaean camp, a structure invisible to mortal eyes. It was the temporary headquarters of the divine allies on our side of the Trojan War, with a strategy room central within it.

They sighed. "He has asked his mother to ask Zeus to punish the Achaeans for dishonouring him."

"How infantile!" I shot up from my seat. "Has Zeus agreed?"

Their solemn silence told me all I needed to know.

Looking away, I felt only despair. "How could he?"

"Reportedly, he was hesitant because he knows you favour the Achaeans."

"As if my opinion has ever meant anything to him!"

"Well, it seems Zeus conceded that he owed Thetis a favour. Something about her saving his throne once upon a time." They gave me a pointed look.

I was furious. "I shall speak with my husband and then with her," I decided aloud, turning for the door.

"I would advise against that, Mother." It was Hephaistos, blocking my path, and who had happened upon our conversation. He looked at me with worry in his eyes.

I scowled at him. "We have a traitor in our midst. Are you suggesting we allow her to be privy to our plans?"

"If you exclude her, she will take Achilleus with her, and we need him if we are to win."

"I agree," Athene spoke up. "The camp is already divided between Achilleus supporters and Agamemnon supporters. We should negotiate with Thetis, give Achilleus back the woman, and get him back on our side."

I did not like it but I saw the wisdom of their words. "So be it."

I glanced back at my son. "Achilleus may be stubborn, but he might listen to his parents."

"Which will only happen if they listen to you," he said. "Which would take a miracle."

"We are gods," I argued. "Miracles are what we do."

"Then I shall accompany you," Hephaistos said. "You should not confront Father alone."

"As you wish."

Zeus sat on his golden throne before the open court.

I pushed through the doors, Hephaistos on my heels.

"Trickster. Is that what the poets should add to your list of epithets?" I called out, my footsteps echoing on the marble tiles.

I stood before my husband. "Must I discover your plans to thwart mine from all but you, my lord? Everyone points out how you support me, choose me above all others, yet today you have proven them all wrong."

"Hera," he sighed. "I will tell you my plans when it is necessary for you to know. Thetis came to me with her request. I knew it would cause trouble for you."

"So naturally, you agreed?" I spat, too infuriated to be polite.

"Check your tone, wife, before you say another word." His face grew dark.

I exhaled heavily, trying to calm down. "My lord, I do not assume to understand the mind of the King of Heaven, or to be as intelligent, but I wish you sought my opinion this once."

"Why would I need it?"

"I raised Thetis. I know her better than most. She has always been the beguiling kind. I bet she grasped at your knees, poured tears from her eyes, and said everything you wanted to hear. Did it occur to you that she may be trying to trick you?"

"Why would she trick me and thwart your efforts?"

"For the same reason that she once offered you her hand!" I sputtered.

He rolled his eyes. "Hera, you must stop this now. I am helping Achilleus, who has been wronged. This is my will. Accept it."

I shook my head as I struggled to understand. "You are aiding our enemies."

"The Trojans are not my enemies."

"They are foreigners who would see your realm destroyed," I pointed out.

"They are part of the human race which I created." Lightning flashed behind his eyes as he spoke.

"Mother," Hephaistos said to me, stepping forward. "We must be patient. Achilleus's absence is but a hurdle which may disappear with time. The war is not lost yet."

"Listen to our son," Zeus told me. "He speaks wisely."

I nodded and held my tongue. It was not over. That was true. As long as Paris was alive, it would never be over for me.

Zeus smiled. "Come, Hera. Let us not quarrel over mortal matters. Drink some nectar. Regain your strength. Rest here tonight. Rejoin the Achaeans tomorrow with a fresh resolve."

He gestured to my empty throne next to his. "Sit."

I obeyed, so that perhaps he would change his mind. I obeyed when he brought me to his bed that night. As usual, he was too drunk to achieve anything. However, I bore what little fumbling he did with as much self-restraint as I could muster, mainly not to beat him around the head with my fists.

The following day, I found Thetis along the sunny, white beaches outside Ilion. She was pacing up and down, dragging one foot through the sand. The other shoved itself through the seawater with every step. When she turned and caught sight of me, she stilled, watching my approach warily.

We stared at each other, locked in mutual hostility.

Despite telling myself to be civil, it was useless.

"Every time I see you, you bring me chaos. So, answer honestly if you can bother yourself: did you join the Achaean forces just to sabotage me?" I demanded.

She chuckled. "Why would you suggest such a thing? Hera, I am on your side."

"Are you? Achilleus would have kept fighting if you had encouraged him."

"Achilleus is protesting against an injustice," she argued. "He made up his mind not to fight before he came to me. As his mother, it is my duty to support him above all else."

I scoffed. "He is having a tantrum like all young men, and his mother is failing to snap him out of it."

"Briseis was his war prize," Thetis replied. "Proof of his achievements."

"Yes, kidnapping, enslaving, and chaining a foreign woman to your bed is a noble accomplishment!"

She shook her head. "Do not lecture me about such things. Do you want to hear how Peleus proposed to me?"

She did not wait for me to reply. "When Zeus decided to marry me off, I put up a fight. The King of Phthia, my pathetic husband, was more than happy to take a goddess for a wife, a nymph queen, no less! Proteus told him where he could find me, how to restrain me, and how to force me to marry him, saying that, according to Zeus, this particular method had worked once on the Queen of Heaven." Her voice broke.

My flame of rage flickered.

She was spitting the words now. "Peleus tied me up so I could not escape. When I tried to change form to get away from him or wriggle free, he pinned me down and took me on the sand. The pain was too much to be able to focus on escape. Afterwards, he compelled me to walk back with him to his palace, knowing I had no choice but to obey. Then he kept me a prisoner in his castle until our wedding. But my humiliation was not complete until you witnessed my husband ravage me again. But I am not your husband. I am not you, either."

Tears began to stream down her face. "Well? Say something!"

I was stunned by her words. "I am sorry for what you suffered."

"On that day, the day before it, or when I was under your care? Which?"

I frowned, confused. "I do not know what you mean. I gave you everything you wanted when you were a child, and you lay with my husband."

"That is a disgusting lie!" she roared, tears trickling down her face. "I had to put up with his disgusting behaviour for years! Do you think I could say no to him? You, the one who was supposed to keep me safe, failed spectacularly. Upon realising what he was doing to me, you had the audacity to wonder if I was to blame. Then you banished me anyway! The truth would have made no difference to you."

"So, why did you come back to Olympos? Why did you try to become Zeus's wife if you so hated him?" I demanded.

"Him I pardoned long ago. All men and gods are driven by lust. It was you I could never forgive. I figured that the one who was supposed to be my mother when I had none would protect me against such monsters, but she did not. It was not Zeus I came for that day, not really."

"And so, you would have gladly been his wife?"

"The satisfaction at seeing you fall would have been enough."

"Speaking as his wife, I somehow doubt it."

"Nothing could be more painful than what you both put me through."

"Enough!" I snapped. "I did not come here to argue over the past. Tell Achilleus to fight."

"I will not," she retorted. "Achilleus will die if he fights. It has been foretold. Do not ask me to send my only son to his death. He is the only good thing I have left."

Although I was enraged with her, I realised that I could not have devised anything worse for her than what she was already going through. I also knew that arguing with my allies would not achieve my goal. So momentarily, I laid aside my anger.

"Would you hate me more if I told you I understand your predicament?"

"You cannot possibly. None of your children are mortal."

"I was referring to your marriage. Would you hate me more if I told you I understand?"

She raised her chin. "I do not know. You must tell me."

And so, I did. I told her my tale of woe.

Thetis listened intently, nodding as she did. She asked me how I tolerated it. We found common ground and peaceful conversation for the first time in years. She spoke of how Zeus had been with her behind my back, how he would touch her under the table, hold her close whenever they embraced in greetings or goodbye, how it began with little brushes, confusing touches so that she did not know if they were on purpose or not. Then it escalated. He would kiss her on the cheeks with simple, light pecks. Then it would be the neck and lips. After that, he would always keep a hand on her, always put his hands in places that felt strange to her at the time. He would tell her about her body, that it was all for him. She would listen and nod, knowing nothing better — I had never taught her any different except how to be obedient. It was horrible to hear how he had used these lessons to prey on her.

I sincerely apologised to her for not seeing it sooner. Thetis apologised for not telling me. I batted her words away, saying that it was entirely my fault. Then we both agreed that the fault, the only blame, lay with Zeus himself.

Then we rested, lying side by side. We spoke of anything but the war. It felt like old times, just for a little while. Then we were roused by the sound of the battle charge and remembered we were at war.

10: ARES

Achilleus's stubbornness had consequences. The following day, King Agamemnon declared that they would make a full-scale attack on the city and that, in doing so, they could take the walls immediately. It was a fool's plan, a scheme of the utmost stupidity. However, as leader of the Achaean army, his men had no choice but to obey. Then suddenly, he changed his mind. In a test of the Achaeans's courage, the King of Mykenai claimed he was giving up the war and returning home to his wife and three children. I knew not whether it was from fear or obedience, but the soldiers eagerly flocked to the ships at the news, ready to board and sail away.

"What in the great cosmos is going on?" I demanded of Athene as we watched the mortals flee from Ilion. "Just now, they were about to attack."

"I know," they murmured.

"If the Achaeans flee, they will give victory to the Trojans, who will forever boast of how they won Helene over her husband. Meanwhile, Ilion is still untouched, with its army intact. Do something!" I commanded, turning to face them. "You are the deity of reason. Go among them and convince them to stay. Make them stand and fight."

Bowing their head slightly, they knew better than to object and muttered a "yes, my lady" under their breath and scurried away, trudging down the cliffside, jumping over the rocks and boulders to carry out their orders.

I do not regret shouting at them. It got the job done.

Athene inspired their favourite hero, Odysseus, to rally the Achaean army and spur them into battle. He reminded them that they swore an oath not to leave the shores of Ilion while the city was still standing.

Both armies in full came to meet. Much to my delight, Paris failed to face his fear and retreated to the back of the Trojan ranks. It showed his true colours: a coward. Yet, he recovered from the scolding he received from his older brother and battle champion, Hektor. Rather than waste the lives of many, a truce had been agreed upon, and he would face King Menelaos of Sparta in direct one-on-one combat.

It was the moment the world had waited for: the two husbands of Helene fighting it out. It was a dogged duel, but how naive Paris was! Did he not realise that a man who had waited so many years for what was rightfully his would be determined to win back his wife? As Menelaos gained the upper hand, inflicting wound upon wound, it was clear Paris was about to be defeated. As I eagerly awaited, I could hardly believe my eyes when Aphrodite flew into the fray, snatched her precious Paris from the ground, and transported him back to his bedchamber where, I am told, he cowered with his wife.

Menelaos left in disgust at the godly intervention. With the reprieve in fighting over, the armies quickly returned to form, sieging and bloody skirmishes, but no victor. Neither would give way.

That evening, Zeus summoned all the gods to a feast on Mount Olympos. He did this many times throughout the war to appear to remain neutral and to foster good spirits between the divided house of Olympos. Athene sat by my side, and we both passed on ideas to each other to further the Achaean gains at Ilion.

Zeus must have heard because he suddenly said aloud, gaining the entire room's attention: "How fortunate the King of Sparta must be to have two Olympian goddesses backing him. On the other hand, Aphrodite desires to keep Paris from Haides's realm. I would say the victory is Menelaos's as he did not abandon the fight, which means the agreement can stand, and Helene can return to her husband. Perhaps both sides can leave each other alone now, and peace can be fostered. What do you say to that, dear wife?"

I pursed my lips at the idea of putting down everything I was fighting for, at the notion that Paris would go unpunished. It was not just the institution of marriage he had insulted but its goddess.

I cleared my throat and replied: "My lord, how can you suggest this when so many have suffered the worst kinds of loss?"

Zeus glowered. "Are you suddenly so understanding of mortal minds? Tell me, how has Ilion insulted you so much that you cannot bear the thought of it standing with its thousands of innocent citizens alive inside? Do you need the Achaeans to destroy the entire royal house of Priam to ensure they will never make another slight against you again?"

"In truth, my lord, I would go to any lengths, betraying even the Achaeans to see that come to pass."

His face darkened. "Hera, I do not wish this war to go on longer than necessary or become a source of strife between us. Yet know this: if I ever choose to destroy a city or people dear to your heart, you better not try to stop me. Of all cities, Ilion is the most precious to me, the most impressive, the most admired by all, and to raze it would be to destroy a great culture."

I clenched my jaw. How could he say that? However, I did not wish to quarrel with him in public, for I would surely lose. So I gave in, slightly. "My lord, I admire your selectiveness, for

I have three favourite cities: Argos, Sparta, and Mykenai, the pride of Hellas for their cultures too. Should you ever choose to bring low any of them, those cities which worship you even more faithfully than all those under Priam's power, I should not cause any fuss."

He grunted and returned to his meal.

Nothing more was said on that matter between us that night.

The Achaeans struggled to gain a decisive victory without the great Achilleus fighting against Hektor and Ares. Amid this disaster, Athene summoned Poseidon and Hephaistos to my tent to discuss the matter. Thetis was absent, so we could not convince her to get her son to pick up his sword again. Word had it that all Achilleus did all day was drink, sleep, play his lyre and lie with his cousin, Patroklos.

Athene's eyebrows furrowed slightly as we looked down on our battleplans. "The other side has abandoned any pretence of following the godly rules of war. They intervene too much with their humans. It leaves us no choice. We must remove any advantages from the Trojans and cut off all their resources, starting with your son."

I blinked. "What?"

"Ares is your enemy now, Hera," they pointed out. "He is the god of war. He must be kept from helping the Trojans. Only then do the Achaeans have a fighting chance. We need to drive him from the battlefield, prevent him from taking part."

"I am inclined to agree with you," I nodded, seeing the sense. "No mother likes to see their son in the fray of battle. It would be for his own good, if nothing else."

"It is not so simple," Poseidon warned me from across the table. "He is Zeus's first-born. You cannot pinch him by the ear and drag him from the battlefield."

"What do you suggest?"

"You need the permission of his father."

Without delay, I hastily sent for my horses and chariot, which had been given to me long ago by Ares himself. The chariot was pure gold, decorated with spirals and the symbols of the gods, and artwork depicting my own sacred animals, the bear, the peacock, and the cow. Its wheels were bronze with iron axles.

Hebe, who had visited the campsite that day to visit me and wish me good fortune in the fight, and to see if she could be of any service to our cause, harnessed the horses with a yoke and bands of gold.

I mounted the chariot alongside Athene, dressed in their father's tunic and battle armour, and helmet, holding their aegis in one hand, depicting Strife and Courage, as well as their shield decorated with the terrifying face of the Gorgon Medusa, with a fishtail and snakes for hair.

We tied our straps of spun silver, and I whipped the horses into motion. They carried us up into the blue sky, under Helios's blazing sun and towards Mount Olympos, where the gates opened for us.

Dismounting, Athene and I found Zeus on a rocky ridge at the city's edge as he looked down across the sea at Ilion in the distance, his fair hair blowing in the breeze.

He did not even turn around to look at us. "What is it now, Hera?"

Though he was not facing me, I knelt. "My lord, I come to you with a request to remove our eldest son, Ares, from the plains of Ilion. Not only does my heart grieve to see my eldest boy in such a place, but justice must also be done for the multitudes of Achaean lives he has taken, those of men who worshipped him. Apollo and Aphrodite wreak havoc upon us, allowing Ares to riot on the battlefield. I hate to see the Achaeans fall in such numbers. Would you be angry if I drove him from the plains of Ilion?"

After some moments, Zeus turned and said, "It is his right to be involved in the fight if he chooses. It is yours too."

Then he fixed his eyes on Athene behind me. "It is good that Athene is your ally, dear wife, possibly the best advisor on this subject. I assume this was their idea. Go now with my permission to do what you must."

Grinning, I got to my feet, ready to wage war on my eldest son, forgetting all affection I had for him, possessed only by hatred for Paris.

Athene and I returned to the cliff edge overlooking the battlefield. It provided a great vantage point from which to see the battle unfold. Both sides had ceased attacks and were regrouping in their respective camps. Ilion was still standing, unfazed by the skirmishes outside its walls. I clenched my jaw at the thought of that coward Paris living safely there. I was determined to end him and his wretched race.

Athene, behind me, said, "Diomedes, the commander of the Argive ships, saw Ares helping the Trojans in battle. He was forced to withdraw his troops, knowing it was a fight that could not be won. Now his men hide in the camp."

"Let us meet this Diomedes then," I said. "These little men give up too easily."

We descended onto the beach and approached Diomedes, surrounded by his comrades, dressed in unbloodied battle gear. At our approach, the men stood ready and bowed in our presence.

"It is shameful to stand dawdling as a soldier," I criticised, "when the Trojans are now attacking your ships, using the absence of Achilleus to their advantage."

Diomedes and his men began to move away, bowing and red-faced, muttering apologies.

"Not you, Diomedes," Athene said.

The lord faltered and remained.

"My ladies, forgive me for not kneeling," he gulped. "I am weary."

"Why should you be weary?" Athene demanded. "You have not been fighting."

"Fighting is in vain when Achilleus withholds his men from battle as Lord Ares leads the Trojans. We face certain slaughter," he said, explaining with a pleading tone. "Have pity."

"Have courage," I corrected him. "Besides, Ares is why we are here. We have a plan."

And so, we told him.

"You wish to take on your own son?" he asked, seeming unconvinced.

"This is war, Diomedes," I told him through gritted teeth. "We do what must be done, but it is also for my son's own wellbeing that I seek this course of action. He must not fight on the side of the Trojans."

"You will prevail, Diomedes," Athene reassured him. "We will be by your side. I will give you a flare of fire from your helmet and another from your shield. You will stand as a beacon to your men."

"I thank you, but how will I be able to fight the gods? Apollo, Ares, Aphrodite — they can all hide from me. Invisible. I will be slain before I even start."

"I shall give you vision to see the gods when they hide," said Athene, as they laid a hand over his eyes. "Use this gift wisely. Aphrodite's son Aineias will be fighting, and she will look to protect him. If she comes into battle, do not fear injuring her. Be brave, and I will protect you."

With such an instruction, Diomedes bowed his head and faced his men.

The Achaeans lined up on one side of the battlefield and the Trojans on the other. Trumpets were sounded, and Diomedes led the cavalry charge from his side, fire blazing from his head and chest, giving courage to his men. Athene and I stayed in the chariot beside him. It bumped along the ground as we charged toward the enemy.

The battle lines slammed into each other, and fighting erupted. Swords clashed and men fell, though more on the side of the Achaeans. The Trojans had Hektor, the son and warrior champion of King Priam of Ilion. The Achaeans did not even have Achilleus.

That was when I saw him. Ares was a spectre amid the raging riot, defeating twelve men with one blow of his sword, the blade long enough to slice an entire troop of men. He removed his sword from the breast of a dead man.

He spotted the approaching Diomedes, who handed me the reins of the chariot and readied his spear. Ares flung his spear at the yoke of the chariot, determined to remove the horses from it and strand us in the middle of the battleground. Athene caught it as it flew and sent it further on its way.

Shocked at the offensive attack, Ares turned with his sword raised high, ready to strike down the mortal upstart. However, the Argive commander released his spear with the help of Athene, who whispered guidance in his ear, flinging it at the god.

It hit him square in the chest.

At the sight of a spear embedded in his body, Ares let out a roar that filled the air and brought everyone on the battlefield to a halt, fearing the sound. My son stumbled back, shocked by the blow. Tears began to run down his face. He looked at me, shocked at the betrayal.

Then turning around, he marched away through the other bloodied men around him. I dropped the reins and jumped to the ground, going after him. Yet it was no use, as he was lost in the crowd.

All was silent on the battleground as the Trojans, and the Achaeans watched the gods of Olympos. Still, my heart was clamouring inside my chest.

Athene's hand was on my shoulder. "Well done."

I pushed them away as tears filled my eyes. "Do not congratulate me."

"Hera, he is your enemy," they replied.

"He is my *son!*"

"You knew what you were getting into," they retorted, annoyed.

"We were only supposed to chase him from the fight. Rout him! Make him flee. Then we could have negotiated," I spat. "The violence was your idea."

"Rout Ares? Such a thing is not possible – he is the god of war. This is his element. He was always going to fight. Do not blame me for his actions!" they snapped in reply. "If you now regret it, that is not my fault. I thought you did not care for him. When have you ever?"

"I do care for him! It is a mother's duty."

"Well, you already failed there long ago."

I fell still and then my hand was slapping Athene across the face.

Crying out, they stumbled backwards. They stared at me, stunned.

Then, clenching their jaw, they said, "Fine. Go after him and bring him back, if you wish to improve our enemy's chances of victory."

Whirling away, they marched back into the battle.

I found Ares in Olympos. I approached him slowly. His entire torso was golden from our handiwork, the top of the spear still sticking out. Of course, he would not die, but perhaps the wound would be there forever.

He halted at the sight of me, fury filling his face. "Father thinks I deserve this. He called me a scoundrel. He scolded me for being a god of war who cannot handle the realities of it, not even when his mother fights against him. However, I must say that I never thought my own mother would plan an attack on me. And yet it is nothing compared to the contempt you have always treated me, though I did nothing to deserve it."

"Contempt?" I was shocked. "Ares, I have loved you like the rest of my family."

He shook his golden head. "Hephaistos was always your favourite. You made no attempt to hide that, especially when you gave him Aphrodite, whom I loved! They say the eldest should be the favourite, but I am not. Even so, how could you do this to me?" His voice cracked with emotion.

All I wanted to do was wrap him in my arms and cradle him as if he was a baby again, mend his wound and turn back time.

"I am so sorry," I whispered, my voice trembling. "For everything."

He was silent for a moment, not looking at me, and then he said: "Do you know what Father said about you just now?"

I shook my head, feeling my heart sink.

"He said you have an indomitable soul, that he cannot control you, and you never give in or stop when you find an enemy." He glared at me. "Am I your enemy?"

I vigorously shook my head. "Of course not."

"I once thought that too," he growled and pushed past me, storming off to find relief for his injuries.

When I heard his footsteps fade, I found myself weak, sinking to the ground for support. I stayed there for a long time, feeling bereft until I resolved to help my son as best I could. He was wounded. He was in pain. That I could help with.

I found Ares lying on a bed in the infirmary under the care of Paean, the palace physician, who had given him ointments after Hebe had washed him clean.

Ares was resting, his head on Aphrodite's lap as she softly caressed his forehead. Hestia knelt by the hearth in the wall, ensuring it heated the room, while Demeter stood at the windowsill, watching the scene.

"Can I help?" I asked, approaching.

"He needs stitches," Paean said, coming forward with his box of instruments. "It shall be painful."

So, I knelt in front of him and took his hand in mine.

Soon enough, Paean sewed him up. Ares screamed, writhing on the bed. It took me, Aphrodite, and a hefty Demeter, who had rushed over, to keep him still. We put a rag between his teeth to stop him from biting his tongue amidst the agony.

When that was over, Paean, Hestia, and Demeter took their leave, leaving Aphrodite and me with my son.

I looked at Aphrodite, my annoyance at her presence dwindling. I had no strength to stay angry while my son lay in pain.

"I can see to Ares," I offered gently. "If you wish to return to Ilion."

She scowled at me. "I care for him just as much as you do."

I noticed a bandage around her wrist. "Have you been wounded?"

She glanced down, and her face grew dark. "Diomedes slashed at me with his bronze blade. I shall be fine. However, I see you have no battle wounds, remaining on the sidelines, watching everyone die for you."

I sighed. "Aphrodite, I have no strength for your insults. You should know that I do not intend to return to Ilion until my son is healed. If you wish to use my absence to your advantage, go now."

She glanced between Ares and me. Then she kissed his forehead and departed the room, closing the door behind her.

I shook my head. While she may have loved Ares, the pride in her victory mattered more now. That was where we differed. Despite my anger, there was nothing more important to me than my children. So, on my knees, I edged closer to my son. He was breathing quietly and unmoving. He was barely aware of me, it seemed. I stayed with him through the night, unable to leave his side.

In the small hours of the morning, with Nyx still outside, he opened his eyes slowly and, upon seeing me in the candlelight, murmured "Mother?"

I tucked a strand of hair behind his ear. "Yes, I am here. Do you want me to fetch Aphrodite, or your father?"

He shook his head slightly. It was barely a movement. "No," he croaked, eyes closing again. "Please, stay."

My heart warming, I did just that. I sang soft songs, told Ares stories, and changed his bandages, even if he was barely receptive to it. I caught up on lost time.

Sitting in a chair in the corner of the room, across from Ares's bed, I looked down at the goblet of mead in my hands. Heaving a sigh, I was about to bring it up to my lips when there was a knock at the door.

Looking up, I saw Athene standing in the doorway. They were still dressed in their armour, their helmet under their arm. One could not see the candlelight reflecting on the metal; it was covered in ichor, mortal blood, and mud. Their usually stern face held a hint of concern.

"How is he?"

"He shall heal in time," I said.

Nodding, they turned to me. "I owe you an apology. I should have never asked you to go against Ares. It was insensitive of me."

"I should have never agreed," I replied.

They blushed. "For the record, I think you have been a great mother to your children, myself included."

"I tried my best," I muttered. "Perhaps for some, it wasn't enough."

"Then that is their problem," they advised. "One cannot do any more than one's best."

I smiled sadly. "Thank you, Athene. Surely you did not come all this way just to apologise to me?"

Athene shook their head. "No. Zeus has summoned the Olympian court. Once Ares is fit to rise from his bed, we must all gather in the courtroom. Zeus has an announcement to make which could potentially turn the tide of this great war."

11: LEUKOLENOS

"I have been blind to the effect mortal matters could have on my own household," the King of the Gods said, sitting on his golden throne at the top of the council table. "I hope I am a fair enough ruler to not control you too much. I hope I allow you to explore the world and let you participate as much as possible as you wish, but there is a limit," he spat, his voice rising. "However, I have had enough. I cannot allow this petty mortal feud to divide my family!"

We all looked at each other with confusion, for we already had been divided by it.

Zeus sighed, clasped his hands together and leaned on the table. "We have our squabbles now and then, as with any family. However, we cannot allow ourselves to be at war with one another. There can never be any problem too grand to divide the House of Olympos. Do I make myself clear?"

No one replied.

"I am forbidding any divine entity who holds sway under the Olympian regime from aiding mortals in the Trojan War."

"Even me?" Ares demanded from further down the table, sounding aghast. "I am the god of war. This is what I do!"

"Yes, boy. Even you," Zeus snapped. "This law applies to everyone."

A tense silence settled on us all.

I glanced around at everyone else, sitting there with quiet anger brewing behind their eyes. Every god present had some role to play so far in the Trojan War. It had become a cause of great importance to each of us. To tell us to distance ourselves from it now seemed incredibly unfair. I silently fumed. There was no way I would let Paris win this war.

"How can we defy this imbecilic new rule?" I demanded, marching through my tent, Athene and Hephaistos on either side of me as we entered our strategy room. "We must be allowed to take part in the war. All of us. It is too much to ask us to be impartial now."

"I agree, Mother," Hephaistos replied. "But we cannot do it alone. We shall need to work with the other Olympians to come up with something quickly."

"Collude with the enemy?"

"Work with those who now want the same thing as you do," he said, turning around to face me. "It is the only way. Zeus cannot punish all of us if we work together, and he certainly could not deny the allegiance of it."

"There is no point," Athene said. "I hear Zeus has just left for Mount Ida, where he will weigh up the chances of victory for each side." They spared us a glance.

Frowning, I dashed to the door to see lightning striking the Achaeans. The Trojans howled in delight, savouring the sight of their enemy being burnt to death by the celestial swords. Those who remained of the Achaeans turned and fled from the battlefield, letting the Trojans win the day.

I huffed in exasperation. "I thought Zeus would remain impartial. The rest of us have to."

Athene shrugged their shoulders. "Apparently not."

I stormed out of the tent and sought the attention of the one man who would do my bidding without question.

King Agamemnon spilt wine onto his lap when he saw me burst into his private tent.

"My lady," he gasped, standing up.

"Your men are dying out there," I told him sternly. "Meanwhile, you sit inside your warm tent, by cosy candlelight, while they give their lives for you."

He shook his head. "No, my lady, of course not. I was just about to join the fight now."

"What fight? There is no fight!" I snapped at him. "The Trojans are winning. We are fleeing like cowards. Your men face disadvantages at every turn and have no one to lead them or rally their spirits. The gods cannot help you now. The Achaeans must help themselves. You must help your men!"

His face grew pale save for his red cheeks, coloured by wine.

"Tell me, why did you bother sailing for this foreign land when you did not intend to bear arms yourself? You came here to take what your subjects would fight for, profit from the risk of their death and ruin, hoping to bring a mighty power down and have your name engraved on the pillars of history while you watched on," I guessed aloud.

He gulped, throat wobbling.

I stared at him in disgust. "Achilleus was right. You are a waste of a man, Agamemnon, and you do not deserve to be a lord of anything, never mind the King of Mykenai."

I raised an eyebrow. "Yet you can still change my mind. Get out there and be the leader you claim to be. Inspire your soldiers. Make them fight to the death as you hoped they would for glory and justice. Tell them to pray to all the lands' gods for their blessing. This war cannot be lost. I will not have it!"

He was trembling in his sandals. There was sweat forming on his brow. He stared at me dumbstruck, frozen to the spot. He did not move on my command.

"Still here?"

He jumped to life, scurrying past me with his head bowed, ready to rally his men.

King Agamemnon stepped up to the mark that day — the soldiers said he was a true leader in times of crisis and despair. He prayed to Zeus, and when the storms cleared and an eagle soared overhead, his men turned right back around and charged the enemy with renewed zeal in their hearts.

"Why the eagle?" Hephaistos asked, as my allies and I watched from a nearby cliff edge. "First, Zeus sends the lightning to kill us, then a bird. For what?"

"To give the men hope," I stated simply, watching the battle closely.

"Our king is constantly changing sides between the Achaeans and the Trojans," Athene said. "Perhaps he does not know what he wants."

"No. You are wrong," I said, still staring at the raging battle below. "Zeus is playing the field, keeping both sides on his. Ultimately he knows that if either believes they have been abandoned by him, they will grow to resent him. Zeus has never been a complete fool."

Narrowing my eyes, I spotted the Achaean hero Teucer among the brawling soldiers, killing one after the other of the enemy. I was hopeful, watching the battle continue in our favour until Hektor injured him and led an effective charge that drove the Achaeans back to their ships.

"Perhaps we should join them. They may need our help," I said.

"You shall do no such thing," a different voice said behind us.

We turned to see Iris, the messenger goddess, standing behind us, with her large golden eagle's wings casting a shadow over us.

"Iris," Athene greeted. "What is it?"

"Zeus thought you might try to re-enter the struggle and has sent me to reiterate the importance of divine impartially in this war," the messenger goddess said.

I blinked at her, taken aback. "He has only just sided with the Trojans!"

"And was it just now your intention to join the Achaeans again?" Iris interrogated us, staring at me intently.

"Yes." Of course, I should have denied it immediately, but I was so incensed by my husband's hypocrisy that I owned up to it with pride. It seemed there was one law for the king and a different one for the rest of us.

"Then follow me, please," Iris commanded, giving us a hard stare before leading the way. "Zeus has summoned you back to Olympos."

I sighed heavily and rolled my eyes. Would he ever stop meddling?

I knelt before my husband, not for the first time, my face red with humiliation and my heart full of rage. I had to shove the words out through my teeth: "My lord, I beg your forgiveness. I was not thinking. When I saw your lightning bolts fire against the Achaeans, I thought it meant that your new law had been cast aside."

"Do not accuse me of betraying the rule I created," Zeus growled, shaking his head, seated on his throne. "I have every right to do so. As King of the Gods, I ensure that the fated victory happens in whatever way I see fit, as long as the Moirai get their desired end."

I raised my chin. "Yet the Achaeans still deserve a chance, my lord."

"I agree, and they will have it. The war will last several more years before it ends," he told me. "The Achaeans will not be crushed now but slowly over time. Only a handful will ever return home."

I refused to give in to defeat. I looked up at Zeus from my kneeling position on the floor. "Then advise me, my lord. I desire your wise counsel," I flattered him, painting on a hopeful smile. "How can I give them that chance?"

Zeus pursed his lips, tapping his fingertips on the armrest of his throne. "I do not feel it to deny you this wisdom, wife. The Achaeans' cause is just. That I will admit. You have removed Ares from the Trojans' struggle, but Hektor is still fighting. Convince Achilleus to fight, and more Achaeans may live to old age than expected."

I nodded, although his words were not what I had wanted to hear.

"That will not be easy," Athene spoke up beside me, speaking my mind. "Achilleus refuses to lead his men into battle because —" they started.

"Because of Briseis being in Agamemnon's tent," Zeus interrupted, huffing. "Yes, I know all about that. He is still young. He will eventually learn better ways."

Maybe not, I thought. "Thetis is convinced Achilleus will die if he fights."

"Such is the risk for any mortal soldier, even a demigod," Zeus said. "There is no reason for him to remain by the sidelines like a coward. Yet you must not fight in this war any longer. If I catch either of you doing so again, the punishment will be severe."

We nodded, and he dismissed us from his presence.

We were not the only ones frustrated with his unfair prohibition. The gods who supported the Trojans were too.

So, a short truce was called in a private meeting chamber in the Olympian palace between the supporters of the Achaeans and the Trojans to discuss what could be done to overturn it and to continue to help our respective forces.

"Why should we help you?" Aphrodite asked, reclining on a chair. "Our side is winning." Her allies surrounded her.

"For now, maybe," Athene answered, who had been elected to lead the diplomatic talks.

Aphrodite scoffed. "If you say so."

"Whether you believe it or not, we all want the same thing," Athene continued. "Fewer lives lost. So this needs to end. A little teamwork could go a long way. To work together would be a tremendous step in the war effort."

I pursed my lips, displeased.

"I think about love a lot, you know," Aphrodite murmured, glancing at the floor. "It has positives and negatives. I find it fascinating how entire cities will go to war over it. Love is a concept which can bring as much pain as pleasure."

No one said anything, wondering where she was going with this.

"Then I had a rather interesting thought," she continued, a grin appearing on her face. "I was going to do it myself, but perhaps it is best if our queen takes the lead on this one."

I frowned. "What?"

Aphrodite stood up from her chair, looking at everyone present. "I think we can all agree that as long as Zeus's watchful gaze scours the Trojan plains, searching amongst the soldiers for any sight of us fighting alongside them, we are in grave trouble. Who knows what the punishment would be for defying him?"

I had a pretty good idea of what it would mean for me.

"Yet what if his gaze was to wander, become distracted?" she asked, as her eyes landed on me. "What if our glorious king's eyes closed, even just for a day? It would give us enough time to offer the Achaeans and Trojans some final long-lasting help before Zeus casts his gaze on them again."

I scowled, cutting through the subtext. "What is it you would have me do?"

She shrugged. "Keep the king distracted."

I narrowed my eyes, my heart beating fast. "How?"

"By doing what wives do best," she chuckled.

My stomach lurched. Never had I felt so betrayed by her. Here she was, in all her malice and vengeance. I knew it was personal this time. She was sending me to him, knowing how things had been for me from the beginning, knowing what he would want to do to me.

"You do not have to do that, Mother," Hephaistos told me, glaring at Aphrodite. "There must be another way to achieve our aims."

"War demands personal sacrifices from everyone who takes part," Aphrodite argued with her ex-husband. "Often unequal and unjust sacrifices."

Then she fixed her eyes on me. "It is time you showed courage, just like the soldiers on the battlefield, overcome your fears, and give your personal contribution to the war effort. Walk into the dragon's den. Or is our queen too cowardly to meet with her own husband on our behalf?"

My head was in a spin. "How can you be certain he will let himself be distracted by me?"

"That's easy. I shall give you my belt, which enchants all around it. You can use the aid of Hypnos. He can hide in the trees and aid you in keeping Zeus at rest for as long as possible. Would that help?"

I nodded. "It might."

She looked me straight in the eye. "So, will you do it, Hera? Best to get it done as soon as possible so that no more humans die than necessary. If not you, I am sure someone else would be willing to do what is necessary for the good of our armies."

"No," I answered, forced into a decision. "I will do it." There was no way I would allow another to crawl into my husband's bed.

So, my seduction of my husband went like this:

First, I went to my bedchamber on Mount Olympos. I readied myself with a bath, rubbing my skin with oil. Then I braided my hair. Afterwards, I dressed in a garment Athene had once woven for me, decorated in beautiful designs of flowers and birds. I pinned it over me with a gold brooch. I put a belt of one hundred tassels around my waist and earrings of three red berries each. Then I placed my veil over my head, put my feet into a pair of sandals, and departed again.

First I went to Aphrodite, who stood outside my bedchamber. She handed me her belt, which would inspire desire in Zeus. It was a breast-belt woven with love, desire, and deception. She assured me that Zeus would do whatever I pleased.

"What reason shall you have for approaching him?" she asked.

I thought for a moment. "I shall tell him I am to visit the house of Okeanos once more. The last time I went, I did so without his permission, and he was angry with me for that."

Then I ventured to Lemnos, where I called upon Hypnos. He was reluctant to come with me as he knew of Zeus's temper. However, he agreed on the condition that I give him the hand of Pasithea, the goddess of relaxation, whom he adored. He called on the gods of the Underworld to witness my promise before the River Styx and only then agreed to follow me to Ilion.

Upon reaching the summit of Mount Ida, from where Zeus was watching the war, Hypnos hid in a tall tree. He took the form of a beautiful singing bird while I approached Zeus. Awkward and shaking, I wondered if he could hear my heart beating as loudly as I could. It did not help.

"Hera. This is a surprise," he said, sounding wary as he heard me approach.

Then he turned to look at me. "You are looking well, my queen."

"Thank you, my lord."

I stood hesitantly. What else could I say? I recalled the excuse for my presence. "My lord, I came to ask your permission to visit the house of Okeanos and Tethys. I fear I have angered you with the recent events at Ilion and I do not wish to hurt you further by disappearing without saying why."

"I don't see why you would go there."

"Apparently, Okeanos and Tethys are experiencing some difficulties in their marriage, and would like my opinion, which I have given them before. Do you mind?"

He smiled. "Of course. You must do your duty."

He cast his eyes out to the battle, distracted.

My heart began to beat faster. I had never had to try to keep my husband's attention before. I was more used to avoiding him.

"I don't have to leave just yet, however. May I join you, my lord?" I asked suddenly.

He glanced at me as if realising I was still there. "Of course."

I stood beside him, hoping the belt would start to work. *Compliment him,* a voice inside my head said. "My lord, I wish to say that you are the bravest of all who have taken an interest in this war."

He blinked at me, seeming surprised. "I suppose so, but why do you think that?"

I gave him my sweetest smile while I had his attention. "You, my lord, have the fortitude to stay impartial and constantly watch over everyone. It must be a great burden. I often wonder how it is you manage. Of course, I do not know how I could, so it is difficult for someone like me to fathom."

Once I said that, Aphrodite's belt did the rest.

Zeus came closer to me, embraced me, and told me how he had never desired anyone more than me. Just to really make me feel exceptional, he started to list the women and goddesses he had ever bedded, some of whose names I had never even known, but how I was more ravishing to him than all of them combined, at that moment. He pressed his lips to mine between each name, his passion mounting. His hands began to rove as his ardour grew. He told me how much he loved my pale skin, calling me leukolenos and saying how heavenly it had always seemed.

I gritted my teeth and prayed it would be over soon.

Hypnos began to weave his spell as Zeus laid me down and undressed me. The warm air around us grew heavy with mist, and the grass became moist with dew.

"Hera, my queen, sleep with me awhile," he mumbled.

"Yes, my lord," I muttered.

I lay my head on his chest, wondering how long I would have to lie there when I felt the gentle tickle of his breath on my ear and heard him gently snoring. I breathed a sigh of relief, thinking my ordeal was over.

12: ACHILLEUS

With Zeus distracted and in a deep sleep, the others returned to the battlefields of Ilion. Poseidon gathered the Achaeans and inspired them to march back to meet the Trojans in combat. He riled up the warriors so successfully that they fought with a new spirit. The mighty Aias even injured Hektor enough to warrant the Trojan's removal from the battlefield behind the city's walls. With their commander gone, the Trojans fell like flies for the first time in a long time.

I watched from Mount Ida, taking comfort in their victory.

Then something happened that I had not expected so soon: Zeus awoke.

I heard his snoring cease, followed by a groggy groan. Looking around, I saw him rubbing his eyes and coming to his senses. My heart was beating fast, and I did not know what to do. He would look down on the plains of Ilion and see the destruction caused by the gods' interference.

"Hera," he said, voice croaky. He got to his feet and approached me. "Still here?"

"Yes, my lord," I replied, turning around to look down on the armies. "I was watching the battle. This mountain is a good lookout. You were wise to choose it as your place of viewing."

He hummed in agreement, putting his arms around me, and leaning his chin on my shoulder. He nuzzled his nose into my neck, sighing slightly, inhaling me.

I was frozen. It was affection I never knew he was capable of, but still, his touch repelled me. I shifted uncomfortably, feeling Aphrodite's belt on my thigh and realising that it must still be having an effect on him.

Then he spoke with a frown in his voice. "Is that Poseidon leading the Achaeans?"

"It seems he has ignored your latest law." I tried to sound concerned. Did I feel bad about betraying my ally? Yes, but I feared Zeus's wrath more.

He removed his arms from my waist.

I turned, feigning confusion.

"That means he is following your orders," he said, eyeing me suspiciously.

My heartbeat quickened. "I do not know what you are talking about, my lord. I do not rule over your brother." Of course, that was a lie. The chain of command had long been established. I was the highest authority when it came to the Achaeans. Being the Queen of Heaven, I had to be.

"Do not try to deceive me, Hera," he warned, his voice hard. He crossed his arms.

I lowered my gaze. "The Achaeans were not being led at all." My voice was shaking.

"So, you chose Poseidon as commander," he finished.

I nodded sheepishly. "Forgive me, my lord."

Thunder entered his eyes.

"How dare you!" he spat. "I told you there would be punishment for your interference. I should smite you into the ground!"

I trembled where I stood. He had only ever been so enraged when I had lost Hephaistos as a baby off Mount Olympos.

Then the rage seemed to slip from his face as he looked at me. "Yet I shall not."

After centuries of knowing Zeus, he still managed to surprise me. After learning about my disobedience, I thought he would pitch me from Mount Ida. Yet he looked disappointed, not angry. I was shocked by his mercy.

He stepped forward and took my hands gently, addressing me in a soft voice. "I take no pleasure in the defeat of the Achaeans, Hera. I want you to know that. I do not take pleasure in a Trojan victory. There is still a chance that Ilion will fall. You may have your justice," he said, reaching up and tucking a stray hair behind my ear. "However, it can only happen if Achilleus joins the struggle."

"Then I will summon him to the battlefield," I said, curtseying and walking away.

"Hera," he called after me.

I turned around, foolishly expecting some half-hearted words of affection or praise.

Instead, he said, "Send Iris and Apollo to me. Then return yourself. Go now."

I did as he commanded and rushed to find my relatives on Olympos. I was greeted by Themis, Zeus's most trusted political counsellor, who offered me nectar to regain my strength before I walked into the courtroom, where the remaining gods of Olympos were crowded.

"Mother," Ares said, coming forward, his brow knitted in concern. "Why are you here? Are you not supposed to be with Father?"

"He knows that we have tried to trick him. Although he has forgiven me, he wishes for Apollo and Iris to go to him immediately." I blushed.

Apollo frowned. "Did he say anything else?"

"Am I in trouble?" Iris asked worriedly.

I shook my head. "I know not. However, I believe he has significant plans for the war."

The two hurried from the room, not tarrying any longer.

Athene glanced at Ares. "You wouldn't know anything about this?"

"Of course not," he snapped. "Since I was banished, the Trojans have made no progress." His hand tightened around the hilt of his sword. "Maybe I should return. If I am cast down by my father, so be it."

"Do not be so foolish," I snapped. "If you do that, Zeus will punish us all. I fear we must wait and see what he wants from Iris and Apollo. Then we shall know how to act."

On Zeus's orders, Iris carried a message to Poseidon, commanding him to leave the battlefield. Meanwhile, Apollo inspired Hektor to take up his sword and lead his men out again. Without a leader, the Achaeans fled in fear at seeing Hektor and Apollo charging them together in Poseidon's absence. The god then magically filled the trenches with sand and mud around the Achaean camp so the Trojans could cross and attack their resources. With Hektor set on burning all the Aegean ships, Patroklos, both the cousin and the lover of Achilleus, entered the fray in his cousin's armour. It was inspirational. How the Achaeans fought! When the Trojans became trapped, the slaughter was immense. Patroklos started to push them back to the city walls.

Night descended on the world. I had returned to Zeus's side on Mount Ida, as he had instructed me. From there, we watched the fighting unfold. Aphrodite's belt was still on my leg. I decided to keep it for a while. It seemed to be my only guarantee of Zeus's mercy.

"Sarpedon," my husband suddenly gasped.

The tall soldier, fighting for the Trojans, was caught in the action against Patroklos.

"Who?" I asked.

"My son," he said, his throat bobbing slightly. "Princess Europa gave him to me."

I blushed, remembering her well.

Zeus continued, "He is fighting for the Trojans, but he shall die if I do not save him."

He shoved past me, about to descend the mountain.

"Zeus!" I called after him. "If you do this, it will only inspire other gods to do the same."

He came to a halt and turned. Looking at the battle, he considered my argument. "You may be right, Hera. You may also be wrong."

Remembering I had Aphrodite's belt on, I walked towards him and brazenly took my husband's hands in mine. "A king must always be just and impartial. You have always known that, my lord. What is the life of one hero against the security of your rule?"

He nodded after some hesitation. "So be it. Sarpedon has his fate. We all do," he said, but he appeared downhearted.

I looked down on the fighting just in time to see Patroklos drive a spear through Sarpedon's heart. I felt the satisfaction of his death from here. Yet, as I left the mountainside, I removed the belt, knowing it was wrong to keep it. It did not belong to me, and its power over my husband only confused me. It was simpler to hate him and to be hated in return.

Patroklos soon died as well. It turns out that wearing a hero's armour does not give one their abilities. Hektor killed him quickly and robbed Achilleus's armour. It was what was needed to get Achilleus back out in the fray — there is nothing quite like heartbreak to cause a desire for revenge. He told his mother he planned to exact vengeance on Hektor for the murder of his cousin. She, in turn, asked Hephaistos to create new armour for her son, along with a specially made circular shield.

Hephaistos spared no detail. A circle of intricate detail decorated the shield, presenting all of civilisation from war and peace to work, love and festivities, and all the cosmos from the earth and ocean to the moon and constellations. This is what Achilleus was fighting for.

Once the armour was complete, I sent Iris to instruct Achilleus to make an appearance on the battlefield as soon as possible, for his presence could not have been more urgent. It was time to show where his allegiance lay.

Achilleus called the Achaeans together. He lay aside his row with Agamemnon, and Briseis was returned to him. Agamemnon called on the army to feed and rest before they returned to battle. Still, Achilleus swore to fast until he avenged the death of Patroklos. Such was Achilleus's rage; he unleashed a bloodbath upon the Trojans. It seemed the war has turned.

I do not know why Zeus had a change of heart. Perhaps he sensed the end of the war was near, and there was not much more the gods could do to prevent the inevitable. Maybe it was the loss of Sarpedon, or perhaps it was the rampage of Achilleus, or maybe it came from the Moirai but suddenly, word was sent from Zeus to all Olympians: the prohibition against the gods' participation in the war was removed.

With no further encouragement needed, all the Olympians descended onto the plains of Ilion. Some were there to watch, others to take part. I remained to direct or help as needed.

Achilleus cut like a scythe through the Trojans, killing one after another. He was about to kill Prince Aineias of Ilion. However, in a move that surprised me, for it caused me to question the loyalty of my allies to my cause to eradicate the house of Priam, Poseidon quickly intervened as it was foretold Aineias would become the king of his people. And so, Achilleus turned away, re-entering the battle with Athene by his side, routing the Trojans with a single battle cry that echoed across the field. With his Myrmidon troops, he pursued them back to the river Xanthus. He killed Lycaon, one of the fifty sons of King Priam of Ilion. It was a bloodbath as they tossed the Trojan corpses into the river. The river god, overwhelmed with the mortal remains in his waters, became embroiled in a fight with him, nearly destroying Achilleus with currents and great waves.

Fearing his death, I sent Hephaistos into the fray. My son set the riverbanks on fire, boiling the water within. The river god begged for mercy and ceased his harassment of Achilleus, who continued his brutal assault on the Trojans. He promised me never to keep the Trojans from harm. With that, Hephaistos and I ceased our attack on the river.

Meanwhile, the gods argued on the sidelines about who would win and when to intervene. Athene crossed words with Aphrodite while Apollo and Poseidon became heated with one another. Apollo wisely opted to yield to the senior god and agreed not to undermine any of his interventions in the war.

Artemis snapped at her twin brother: "So you would hand over victory to that lot? If that be the case, never again let me catch you bragging about your skills with a bow if you refuse to use the damn thing."

Annoyed, I grabbed her wrist. "Listen to me. You may be the best huntress but do not threaten those who might make peace, or we shall see who is strongest."

Artemis snorted. "You? I have seen how you flinch in a fight. Why should I fear you?"

Incensed by her insolence and already frustrated on the sidelines as the war reached its most critical moment, I wrenched her bow from her shoulder as she cried out. Then, in a blind fury, I beat Artemis with it. She fell to the ground, crying out for mercy and aid. But I did not stop. No one stopped me, either. All were shocked at the sight of me hitting the maiden. But I did not care. Soon Artemis's arrows fell from her quiver as she struggled under the blows. When I ran out of strength, I tossed down her bow. Getting to her feet, Artemis's face was wet with tears. She looked around at the crowd and took off on her heels, her cries echoing in the wind. Unbothered by her sobbing, I looked back upon the fight.

Achilleus was facing Agenor, a Trojan prince, in single combat. Agenor threw his spear, but it fell low and rebounded off Achilleus's armour. Achilleus showed no mercy on the unarmed prince, springing forward, ready to find his mark. At that exact moment, Apollo shrouded Achilleus in a mist and whipped Agenor away before returning, disguised as Agenor, leading Achilleus towards the city gates where Hektor stood. Achilleus could not see he was being led towards Hektor by Apollo, where I assume the god hoped Achilleus would meet his end.

Hektor remained alone at the city gates to face Achilleus as the Trojans fled back within the city walls. At first, the Trojan champion attempted to negotiate with Achilleus, but ditched this effort upon the realisation that Achilleus swore to kill him and nothing else. Then, out of nowhere, Hektor fled. It was a shocking sight. For the first time in his life, the Trojan champion became a coward. Achilleus chased him around the walls of Ilion. Apollo, seeing his man flag, gave him the power to ensure he stayed in the lead. Three times they circled the city walls.

I sent Athene to intervene.

From having started the war not wanting to interfere, the goddess did not hold back. They knew this combat could decide the victory. Athene took the form of Hektor's brother, Deiphobus, and teased him that he was a coward. Achilleus wasted no time as Hektor stopped running to face his brother.

He flung his spear at Hektor, but it missed its mark. Now provoked into action, Hektor decided he must fight. He threw his spear, but it hit Achilleus's great shield.

Meanwhile, Athene had donned the helmet of Haides, which made her invisible and ran to retrieve Achilleus's fallen spear. At the same time, Hektor turned to his brother to ask for his weapon, to find Deiphobus had vanished. Hektor's face dropped. He knew he had been duped. Pulling his sword, he faced Achilleus, now re-armed with his spear. However, Achilleus knew the chinks in Hektor's armour, for it was his own, that which was stripped from Patroklos's body.

Hektor faced his doom.

Achilleus showed no mercy; such was his hunger for vengeance for the death of Patroklos. Effortlessly, he sliced the Trojan prince through the throat. Dropping to his knees, blood gushing out from his neck, Hektor croaked out a plea for his body to be honoured in death. But Achilleus's revenge was not over. First, he let his hounds eat at Hektor's flesh after the gods abandoned their protection. Then, slitting the heels of the body, he tied the body to his chariot and dragged it back to the Achaean camp. The soldiers all took turns stabbing the corpse. Then Achilleus dragged it around the walls of Ilion before the eyes of King Priam and Queen Hekabe and all the citizens who looked on in horror, as well as many of the gods who squabbled among each other at the injustice of such treatment.

I admit that I was impressed. It was an act of revenge worthy of me.

Later that night, Zeus sent for Thetis, who had fled the campsite. Iris found her hiding in a cave, weeping with her friends, unable to watch the battles now that her son had once more rejoined the fighting. Iris escorted her to Olympos, where the gods welcomed her back to her old home, including me, who gladly handed her a cup of nectar and informed her that Achilleus was very much alive and had brought our victory in sight, having killed Hektor. He had cut the dragon's head from its body, and now the Trojans were without their hero.

Meanwhile, on Earth, King Priam supplicated Achilleus secretly and begged for his son's body to be returned to him. The Achaeans allowed the Trojans twelve days of mourning for their lost prince. However, despite Hektor's death, Ilion's army was still somewhat intact. The city's tall walls remained unbroken, with Paris still safely inside.

13: ALEXANDROS

Athene called me to a meeting. Visiting their temple at Olympos, I ventured into their war room. I found my other allies there: Hephaistos, Poseidon, and Thetis.

"My lady," Athene said, rising with the others at my entrance. "Thank you for joining us. Please, sit." They gestured to the empty seat before the table.

I sat between Hephaistos and Thetis, wary as I did not know what conversation was about to ensue.

The others sat after me.

Athene clasped their hands. "The Trojan War has dragged on for ten years, as you all know. Both sides have lost thousands of soldiers. It cannot go on like this."

"You are not about to suggest surrender or retreat, are you?" I asked.

"Absolutely not. Matters are not that desperate."

I breathed a sigh of relief.

"However, if the Achaeans fail to penetrate Ilion's walls in a year or two, we may be forced to surrender or retreat. We are losing; I think we can all agree."

Everyone else nodded. The harsh reality was very concerning.

"So, the time has come to consider something else. The face-to-face battle will not work against the Trojans anymore. With Hektor gone, they hide behind their walls like cowards rather than face Achilleus in front of our army. They are holding out well despite our siege and the Achaeans destroying the nearby cities, including all crops and animals. But we have limited provisions and men remaining. Neither will survive forever.

Morale is fading. The soldiers could likely mutiny and return home. Whatever we decide today must ensure the destruction of Ilion's walls. It is the only way to ensure victory and make this whole decade of death worthwhile."

"Well, you are the battle strategist among us. I assume you have a suggestion," I said, impatient to hear the solution.

"As it happens, I have something special in mind." With a grin on their face and cunning in their eyes, the deity of wisdom told us their plan.

The wooden horse, a vision of Odysseus inspired by Athene, was constructed in three days as the final military move for the Achaeans to take Ilion. Inside, thirty soldiers had climbed. The rest of the Achaeans burned their camp to the ground and loaded their remaining ships with all the possessions and war slaves they could fit on board. Then they sailed for Tenedos, where they waited for the signal of fire, leaving the wooden horse behind, with a volunteer to help deceive the enemy, to be later found by the Trojans.

The Achaean warrior Sinon claimed to have been abandoned and forgotten by his countrymen, who had given up the war. He pleaded for his life, saying the horse was a peace offering to both the Trojans and Athene for pursuing an unjust war and to bless their homeward journey.

Many Trojans suggested bringing the horse inside the city. But the Trojan priest Laocoon spoke out, advising them against the action. As they debated amongst themselves, listening to the rousing words of the priest, Poseidon grew impatient, fearing the ruse would be discovered. He sent two enormous sea serpents to strangle the priest and his sons. The Trojans were terrified of this omen and what Athene might do should they not accept the offering. So they decided to bring the wooden horse inside their walls and rejoice, not listening to Kassandra, Hektor's sister and priestess of Apollo, who prophesied that such action would destroy the city. It had been unfortunate for her that she had been cursed by Apollo to always speak accurate predictions but to never be believed. But, happily for us, once again, she was ignored.

Under the dead of night, as the citizens of Ilion slept after their celebrations, the city falling silent, the Achaeans left the wooden horse at the beckoning of Sinon. They opened the gates and lit the beacons, summoning the Achaean army to their victory. The Trojans were slaughtered. Ilion was burned alive from the inside out.

"It is heart-breaking, destroying the walls that I helped build, even though I was enslaved," Athene sighed sadly as we looked down from high at the city bright with fire, the air filling with smoke and screams. "We all helped build them."

"I did not," I replied, staring at the falling city.

I descended upon Ilion, keen to see its end for myself. Entering the broken gates, I moved past the burning houses, invisible to the panicked citizens and their attackers. I stepped over blood-covered cobblestones, dodging flying roof tiles, missiles, and angry sword swings. The palace of Priam lay in the distance on a hill. I walked towards it, seeing its large double doors had been beaten down by force. Zeus had been right. All it had taken was for the walls of Ilion to fall — walls built by the gods themselves — for Priam's great empire to collapse in one fell swoop.

I saw figures running out of their homes, their clothes aflame. I saw women being tossed out onto the streets, beaten, and raped before having their throats cut, while some received the reverse. Possessions thrown out of windows, and Achaean soldiers terrorised old men and women who could not fight. I saw them flay a man — several held him down while several more skinned him. Those who were left alive were screaming over the bodies of their dead lying in the streets.

Then I saw the wooden horse ablaze in the town square. Who had set fire to it, I knew not. Trojan soldiers battled the Achaeans in their streets, the ambushes led by brave local men with no armour, having just woken from their beds to die at night. I saw one of the Trojans don the armour of a dead Achaean, only to be killed by his own countrymen, mistaking him for a foreign invader. Men were throwing each other from the roofs of the houses. Others hanged themselves from their windows.

I entered the palace, and the scenes were much the same. Hellenes looted and pillaged the grand building, all the gold, silver, jewels, and women they could lay their hands on. Queen Hekabe was among them, an old woman, dressed in royal finery with a haughty look in her eye.

I went up the marble steps, peering into the open doors of the great throne room. I saw the son of Achilleus, Neoptolemus, standing before King Priam on the altar to Zeus. Dressed in his battle armour, the king had been protecting the last of his family. It was a weak fight. Priam, being old, did not fight hard. Perhaps he knew that defeat was before him. Neoptolemus quickly threw the old man to the ground. In his last effort, Priam cast his spear from his prone position. It did no damage at all, bouncing off the Achaean's shield. As a final insult, Neoptolemus slew Priam's sons and grandsons and beat Priam to death.

I moved past the throne room to an enormous hall of staircases. From one, I saw Paris shoot down Achilleus, an arrow darting into his heel, the weakness of his invincibility.

Achilleus collapsed, roaring so loudly that dust fell from the ceiling. Then Paris shot another arrow into the great hero's heart. Staring wide-eyed up at the ceiling, the light passing from Achilleus's eyes, wheezing out his last breath, he joined the world of the dead.

Almost immediately afterwards, Paris took a poison arrow in the back from an Achaean archer, Philoktetes, on a high balcony behind him, facing the hall of staircases. Philoktetes had once been a friend of Herakles and inherited the hero's poison arrows which now pierced Paris's heart and lungs.

The prince's limbs went lax. He glanced down at the arrows in mute shock and pain. He met my eyes briefly. Then, falling forward over the railing, he tumbled to his death, landing on the concrete floor below next to the body of Achilleus. His blood, guts, and brains flew far and wide, decorating the walls around him.

I relished the sight of it. Paris was finally dead.

A scream echoed from above.

I saw Helene's golden locks as she looked down, having witnessed her lover's death.

At the sound of her voice, an Achaean soldier below, with a troop of companions, bellowed, "There she is! Seize her!"

They raced up the stairs after the Queen of Sparta.

Helene tried to flee with Andromache, the widow of Hektor, but their escape did not last long. Andromache was captured and brought to the house of Menelaos as a slave to serve his daughter, Hermione. Helene was found a few days after her flight from the palace, having taken refuge with other Trojan royals. It is said that she had a wedding ceremony with Deiphobus, Paris's younger brother. I do not know if this is true. If so, it was a short and unhappy marriage, for rumour had it that, when the Spartans found them, she hid

Deiphobus's sword so he would die. She was then taken prisoner by her husband's forces.

At first, I savoured the sight of the destruction. However, as I saw the families destroyed, wives raped by Achaean soldiers, the glee was sapped from me bit by bit. I realised the true horror of what the Olympian gods, myself included, had visited upon the city of Ilion. I reminded myself that this was the price of separating a royal couple in Sparta — the Achaeans were simply repaying the crime a hundred times over. Nevertheless, it did not sit well with me to watch the calamities unfold, and I hurried from the palace back through the streets of Ilion.

Bodies had begun to pile up in the gutter. Many had been cast into the belly of the burning wooden horse to make space. Some were defiling the corpses themselves, while more had set ablaze other piles of bodies to ensure they were dead. Those that had not entirely passed away perished in further agony.

Disgusted, I carried on to the gates of the city. The few thousand who had survived the city's collapse were spilling out simultaneously. Some people raced for the sea, lugging boats between them. Some chased after them, desperate to flee with them. Yet more headed for the hills, taking their chances by land. I saw a young man carrying his aged father on his back, holding onto his little boy's hand. It was a desperate sight of screaming, tearful faces. Even when I had returned to the Achaean ships, Ilion kept burning. The fire ate all there was until the wooden beams of the houses collapsed, and the stone caved in, leaving the city as a pile of death and debris.

The world was shocked at the Achaeans' victory. While there was mass relief that the war was finally over, many were angered that the chivalry of traditional warfare had been cast aside. Many more despaired at the extent of Ilion's destruction.

However, they rejoiced in their victory, ignoring how it came about, for they could return home. The Spartans returned home and honoured me with the title Alexandros, meaning the 'protector of men'.

For those in Heaven, the end of the war was a joyous blessing. Divisions could heal. The family could reconcile. Peacetime could begin.

14: MENELAOS

Ilion was still in flames days after the Achaeans entered the city. After slaughtering every soul that they could see and stealing as much Trojan gold and silver as possible, they returned to the camp and began to hold celebratory games. At the same time, the more impatient commanders started to consider how to get home.

Athene and I sat with Agamemnon and Menelaos in Agamemnon's royal tent. The two brothers were sitting side by side, now lords over the Troad region of Phrygia, Sparta, and Mykenai. They had been deciding how exactly to divide up their victories.

Suddenly, the flap to the tent opened and a troop of soldiers, blackened with ash, marched in. Behind them, they dragged Menelaos's wife, Helene.

Seeing her, we all shot to our feet.

Bound and gagged, her golden locks were dirty and matted. She was wearing a flimsy white robe wrapped around her shoulders, like a sheet taken from her bed, as if she had just been dragged out of it. However, her aquamarine eyes shone brilliantly from her diamond-shaped face. She was just as beautiful as she had been as a maiden, now a woman in her mid-thirties.

"My lords," the troop captain announced as the guards dropped her, her shackles banging as she fell to the floor. "We have brought you Queen Helene of Sparta."

"Helene of Ilion, you mean," Agamemnon said, glaring at her. "She chose to abandon her husband, home and people for another."

I glanced at Menelaos. He was standing back, staring at her with wide eyes. Every muscle in his body was tensed, but his facial expression was blank.

"Husband," Helene croaked, looking up at him. "Forgive me."

Agamemnon spat on her cheek. "Do you think you have any right to address him or any of us after what you have done?" he roared.

Helene recoiled, turning her face away. Her shoulders were shaking as she wept silently.

Agamemnon regarded his brother. "She deserted you, was unfaithful to you and watched from those bloody walls while our men died fighting to protect your honour and punish the insult made to your house, which she shamed. She must die."

Alarm seized me. I looked at Athene in shock, but they seemed unmoved. Was this the plan all along? I had thought the Spartan campaign to Ilion had been a rescue mission, not a hunt.

Menelaos nodded, still in some kind of trance. Then he unsheathed his sword from his side, the sound causing Helene to gasp as she shivered on the floor. The blade was long and sharp. It would cleave her apart in one go if Menelaos chose to be merciful.

I rushed forward. "King of Sparta, are you certain this is the action you wish to take?"

Menelaos gulped, glancing at his wife.

Agamemnon bowed his head to me, jaw clenched. "With all due respect, my lady, it would be folly for Menelaos to keep the wretch alive and bring her back to Sparta as his queen. The people would hate her. She has cost thousands of lives. To allow her to go unpunished would be a terrible idea."

"I agree she should be punished. As you said, the people would hate her. Returning her to her previous life would be her punishment, to spend the rest of her days despised and scorned. She would have no peace, no friends, and no love. Is that not what she deserves?"

Menelaos gripped his sword harder. "How do I know if her next child will be mine? How do I even know if the children she gave me are mine? What if she has never been faithful and never will be?" he asked, his voice quiet and deadly, looking at Helene with fury.

I glanced at her, examining her body. "She is not pregnant. Taking Helene back as your wife might seem merciful, even weak. But the world's hatred of her would be misery enough that she would wish for death every day."

"On the other hand, you, little brother, do not deserve to endure her presence," Agamemnon argued, addressing Menelaos. "Remove her from your life now. Go home and find a new, young, pretty, sweet, and sensible wife who will honour her marriage vows. Perhaps no one will be as beautiful as this one," he gestured to Helene, "but we have seen what beauty can do. We are better off without it."

Menelaos nodded and looked at the guards. "Hold her down."

They knelt, gripping her.

Helene screamed for mercy and pity, begging him not to execute her, wailing like a wounded cat. Tears streamed down her beautiful face. She reminded me of Aphrodite when she asked me about her marriage to Hephaistos, a fate she feared.

My heart sank. I had argued for Helene's life. There was not much more I could do.

Menelaos stood beside her, leaning on his sword, his eyes closed in prayer.

"Any last words?" Agamemnon sneered down at her.

Helene shook her head, choking on her sobs.

"Whenever you are ready, brother."

Menelaos took a deep breath and swung his sword, raising it high.

I winced, bracing myself.

However, the sword never swung down on her neck. Menelaos held it there, staring at Helene in confusion.

Her sobbing had caused the sheet around her shoulders to slip, pooling around her legs, revealing her unblemished white skin beneath. Although on her knees, the curves of her body were entirely visible. There was nothing old or misshapen, despite her age or the fact that, in her lifetime, she had given birth to nearly ten children combined in her separate unions. Still, her skin glowed, young and bright, with the divine aura of her father, Zeus.

So it was that Menelaos dropped the sword. It clanged against the floor.

Helene jumped in fright, staring up at her husband in shock and disbelief.

Menelaos looked at his brother. "I cannot," he whispered.

I sighed, relieved.

"Then, I will," Agamemnon offered, stepping forward.

Menelaos shook his head and waved him away before gesturing for the guards to let Helene go. Confused, they obeyed.

The King of Sparta stared at his queen with disappointment. "Get up," he said.

Helene scrambled to her feet and stood before him, naked, her head bowed.

Agamemnon shook his head. "You are a fool, little brother." Then he stormed from the room, pushing past the guards.

"Redeem yourself," Menelaos growled at his long-lost wife. "Before I change my mind."

I raised an eyebrow, noting Helene did not attempt to cover herself, despite shivering.

"My lord," she began, trembling as she gave him a pleading look. "What has injured my spirit above all else was being unable to return to you, not the bloodshed I have caused, nor your anger at me."

She cast her eyes downwards, and a tear trickled down her cheek. "When he came to Sparta, the prince from Ilion beguiled me as much as he did you, my lord. I trusted him because I thought that if my lord husband put his faith in a foreigner and welcomed him into his house, I would surely be all right to follow him."

She raised her eyes to Menelaos, blue irises shimmering. "At one moment, I was on the docks, speaking with him with nothing to fear. Next, I was locked in his cabin. There was nothing I could do to escape. By the time we reached Ilion, I was already his."

Menelaos clenched his jaw and looked away.

She sobbed, not holding back her tears now, her shoulders shaking. "I never felt lesser than at that moment, taken away from everything and everyone I knew and loved, my husband, my children, my country, and forced to be a slave to the will of another whom I barely knew, compelled to be a mother to children I hated. The only way I could sleep at night next to Paris was to imagine I was back at home, lying next to you. Every day I mourned the loss of Sparta's fields, the comforting touch of my husband, and the faces of my children with him."

Then, sniffing, she started to smile. Despite her rugged appearance, it only made her more beautiful. "When I heard that you were coming to Ilion, I thought it was to my rescue. I was so happy. When I saw you challenge Paris on the battlefield, I stood on the battlements and cheered, not for the Trojans, but for you. When Paris fled the field, I was disgusted by how weak and cowardly he was and angry at myself for not seeing it sooner. Now, your hatred of me, of what you think I did, makes me feel lower and more afraid than I ever have before in all my life."

Menelaos stared at her.

I held my breath. It was impossible to read on his face what he was thinking.

Then, Menelaos took off his cloak and wrapped it around her shoulders, holding her close to him. He kissed her gently on the forehead. "Do not fear me, my love. To be wed to such a loyal and loving wife, not just one so beautiful, has made me the happiest and most fortunate man on earth."

Helene looked up at her husband with wide eyes, and her mouth parted. I wondered whether she was amazed at her husband's forgiveness or was simply relieved that she was still alive.

Then Menelaos kissed his wife, and they fell into each other's arms.

As the goddess of marriage, my heart filled with joy. I felt justified for persisting in righting the terrible wrong that had been done to them both. It had been right to support the Achaeans.

The King of Sparta returned to Lakonia with his queen. The public's reaction to her return was one of abhorrence. They hated her for depriving their nation of two generations worth of soldiers. The women at court shunned her. There were calls for her execution, but Menelaos would not hear of it. Their children finally got to know their mother once more.

However, Hermione, Helene's daughter, would despair in her letters to her betrothed, Prince Orestes, the son of Agamemnon, saying that the only reason she remembered Helene was her mother was that hers was the most beautiful face when they had departed the ships at the dock; while it was said the only reason Helene knew Hermione was her daughter was that someone told her. As Hermione grew older and gained a household, she took her frustration out on her war-slave Andromache, Hektor's widow.

Meanwhile, Helene lived out the rest of her days in relative isolation, a distant figure in the palace, keeping to her chambers and her husband's bed and not venturing too far from it. If she did, the courtiers would drag her out to the town square, where the public would beat her for her crimes against them.

When I remember how Menelaos embraced his wife, I knew that Aphrodite, for all her beauty, had never been more wrong, that any deaths, at the end of the day, were on her head, not mine.

15: AGAMEMNON

Everywhere was fascinated with this tale of love and hate. There was not one land, realm, or kingdom that did not know of Helene, Paris, Achilleus, Priam, Agamemnon, Menelaos, and Odysseus. Homer himself took advantage of the great attention now on Ilion and Mykenai. He created his famous songs that would echo for millennia to come.

However, the Trojan War was not over for the people who fought in it, nor for my role in their tales. I must finish their stories, starting with Agamemnon, King of Mykenai. To understand his future, one must return to his past, a history full of duplicity and betrayal, of crimes most heinous.

The sons of Atreus, Agamemnon and Menelaos were known as the Atridae. Atreus was a son of Pelops and grandson of Tantalos. Tantalos was a son of Zeus and a nymph called Plouto.

Years ago, around the time when Demeter's daughter Persephone had been kidnapped by Haides, Zeus had announced his son Tantalos's birth. Did I take specific action against Plouto or her bastard? No. At that stage, I had accepted that Zeus was a serial philanderer and faithless in his marriage vows, and there was nothing I could do to stop him. I was exhausted by the regret of such previous actions.

Tantalos had a kingdom south of the Troad region in Phrygia. He had invited the gods to an evening midsummer feast at his house, which was large and gaudy, as suited a son of Zeus. The man himself was large, fat, and bearded with greying hair. He bore his father's sharp, silver eyes and carried the same smirk on his lips.

The son of Zeus greeted us at his great double doors, arms splayed, neglecting to bow to his father. He then led us through his massive stone house through the main hall and outside to a large paved courtyard overlooking the mountains beyond. He had placed his own throne at the head of the table and invited Zeus to sit at his side.

The table was heaving with silver platters filled with various foods, including delights from the eastern shores of the Aegean Sea, from places such as Lydia, Ionia, and Lykia. His own son, Pelops, had travelled a lot, bringing many delicacies to his father's home. Eager to taste the delights of the Anatolian world, we all happily sat down. I could see the look of displeasure on Zeus's face, his bare tolerance of the lack of deference, and a growing dislike towards his son as the evening progressed, but he held his tongue.

When I remarked on the predominantly female presence among his slaves, who were serving us, Tantalos roared in laughter and said he had always preferred the company of women, boasting of his polygamy and preference for his daughter, Niobe, over his sons, Pelops and Broteas.

Then conversation broke out between the diners. I tasted the stew's juices as I listened to Zeus and Tantalos in conversation. It was hot and brothy, with a strange taste.

"Where are my grandchildren these days?" Zeus asked.

"Niobe is to be wed to Amphion, as we discussed," Tantalos told his guest of honour.

"Who is Amphion?" I asked.

"You will not have heard of him," Zeus told me. "He is my son by Antiope. Amphion and his twin brother, Zethrus, founded the city of Thebes."

"I thought that was Kadmos." I felt discombobulated. *Zeus had another two sons somewhere?*

"Yes, Kadmos founded the community and created the citadel, but Amphion and Zethrus built the walls. Do keep up, Hera." He turned back to Tantalos. "What of Pelops and Broteas?"

"Broteas has recently distinguished himself as a hunter, and Pelops is here tonight." Tantalos grinned and continued to eat his meal.

The table fell silent as we all looked around in confusion.

Demeter, not listening, grabbed a joint of meat from the central roast and carved it up from the beast on the platter, a beast I could not recognise among any animals I knew of.

Glancing down at my own stew, from which I had taken a sip of the juices, the sicker I felt. I knew it looked odd. I knew it was unlike any other meat I had tasted.

Realising the truth, I spat my mouthful onto the bowl. Then I seized my goblet of wine and washed it down my mouth before slamming it back down on the table.

"Do not eat it," I choked out, my throat still recovering.

It took a few moments for the grim reality to sink in for Zeus.

Demeter, eyes still red and puffy from crying over her loss of Persephone to Haides, made a confused noise in my direction, her mouth still full.

"Spit that out!" I cried.

Her eyes widened. Then, she turned away and vomited onto the floor.

Tantalos started chuckling as realisation struck the rest of the guests, who glanced with mounting horror between their food and their host.

My husband pushed his chair away from the table and stood up. "Are you mad?" he roared at Tantalos.

Clouds brewed overhead, and lightning flashed outside.

His son's giggling grew more alarmed, as did his face when he realised the wrath he had unleashed upon himself. He quickly resembled a blubbering babe.

Zeus's thunderous voice filled the halls: "May you never feel the satiation from the touch of others, the taste of food, or the sweetness of wine. May you never again feel the joys of satisfaction. For the sacrifice of your son, you shall endure eternal torment in the Fields of Punishment. I vow to make sure that my brother Haides carries out such a sentence on his nephew and my son, of whom I have never been so ashamed."

Tantalos was cast down through the earth to the Underworld, Zeus's curse going with him. Persephone later told her mother how Tantalos was tortured by the Furies in the Fields of Punishment for his sins against nature. Standing under an apple tree for eternity on the banks of the River Styx, he could never reach high enough to eat the fruits above him nor stoop low enough to drink the water below.

Afterwards, Pelops was raised from the dead by the Moirai, who let him have a second life. His body was restored, but his left shoulder, which Demeter had been so unfortunate in her grief as to bite into, was replaced with one of ivory. Then he was brought to Olympos to stay in the court during his youth, so he could learn how to be a good king. Once he had grown into his manhood, there was, like many others of his age, the idea of marriage. He had fallen in love with Hippodamia, the most beautiful woman of her age. She was the daughter of King Oenomaus, who had claimed the Kingdom of Pisa, on the far west peninsula, in the south of Hellas, for his own.

However, Oenomaus was haunted by a prophecy that he would be killed by his son-in-law. So each suitor who came for the hand of Hippodamia he had killed by challenging them to chariot races, which were far bloodier affairs than one might first imagine. When the rider's blood was pumping, the audience cheering and jeering, and the speed building, it was not unusual for the horses to teeter out of control, and fatal crashes became almost standard. In fact, Hellenic culture grew to expect death at most sports games it held. Chariot racing was no different. After killing off his daughter's suitors, Oenomaus affixed their severed heads to the palace walls. One could imagine Hippodamia's disillusionment with her father's behaviour. Whenever she found a possible match to avoid dying an old maid, her father took him from her; he who should have wanted it most for daughters who were often a significant burden for fathers.

In order to win Hippodamia's hand, Pelops prayed for Poseidon's help in the chariot race against Oenomaus. The god granted Pelops winged, untamed horses to drive his chariot. Then Pelops sought the help of Myrtilos, a son of Hermes, in return for half the Kingdom of Pisa and Hippodamia's maidenhead on his wedding night, when he won the race.

Myrtilos agreed, and the night before the race, he sabotaged the chariot of Oenomaus by replacing the bronze linchpins of the chariot axles with ones of beeswax. When Oenomaus raced and the wheels heated up, the wax melted, and the chariot fell apart. The King of Pisa was dragged around by his horses, who did not stop racing until his death.

Then Pelops killed Myrtilos by pushing him over a cliff into the sea when Myrtilos attempted to rape Hippodamia. Still, as Myrtilos fell into the rocky sea, he uttered a curse on the line of Pelops. Pelops took Hippodamia's hand in marriage and became the new King of Pisa, holding funeral games in Oenomaus's honour and beginning the tradition of the Olympic Games. Some say Hippodamia knew Pelops's plot from start to finish and even made a deal with Myrtilos herself.

Some claim she married Pelops blissfully unaware that her husband had once promised Myrtilos her maidenhead. Either way, their marriage was successful, as they had two sons, Atreus and Thyestes. Pelops also had an illegitimate son called Chrysippos, who was killed by Atreus and Thyestes on the order of Hippodamia. At any rate, Pelops banished Atreus, Thyestes, and Hippodamia north to Mykenai. Hippodamia hanged herself in shame and grief.

Atreus, after promising Artemis his best lamb as a sacrifice, instead found among his flock a golden lamb which he gave to his wife, Aerope. She then passed it on to Thyestes, with whom she was having an affair. Thyestes then came to his brother and said that whoever had the golden lamb should be King of Mykenai. Atreus readily agreed, believing the lamb to still be in his keeping and not realising the betrayal of his wife. However, when Thyestes revealed he possessed the golden lamb, Atreus was forced to be subservient to his brother. Atreus turned to Zeus, his great-grandfather, for advice. Not pleased with the injustice, Zeus sought Helios's help. Atreus got Thyestes to agree that the throne should be his if the sun rose in the west and set in the east. Thyestes, considering this to be an impossibility, agreed. Little did he know that Helios stayed put that night and, in the morning, set out from the west.

Atreus retook the throne of Mykenai and quickly learned how Aerope and Thyestes had an affair. Like his grandfather, he served his family for dinner, killing Thyestes's sons and presenting them to his brother as a meal. Thyestes did not realise the trick until it was too late. To make matters worse, he was banished from the kingdom for consuming human flesh.

Thyestes made the most of his travels. He visited the Oracle of Delphi, who informed him how revenge on Atreus could still be his: sire a son with Pelopia, his own daughter, who would kill Atreus. And so, when Pelopia was washing her clothes in a river near Sikyon in northern Sparta, she was attacked. Quick-witted, she managed to gain his sword, which she intended to keep to identify her assailant later, swearing vengeance.

In the meantime, Atreus had divorced Aerope for her treachery. He came to Sikyon and, mistaking Pelopia, his niece, for a daughter of the local king, Thesprotos, asked for her hand in marriage. Thesprotos agreed to the union to avoid revealing an even worse truth about Pelopia's already delicate condition. She soon gave birth to a son, Aegisthus, whom she abandoned, with the sword of her attacker, in shame of the true nature of his birth. However, a shepherd found the infant and gave it to Atreus, who adopted and raised him as a foster father.

By this time, Atreus already had two sons, Agamemnon and Menelaos. The two youths hunted Thyestes from his exile in Delphi. They brought him to Atreus for execution, to be performed by Aegisthus with the sword given to him by Pelopia. He met with Thyestes, who recognised it.

Pelopia was sent to clarify matters. Once she realised that her father had raped her all those years ago, she stabbed herself with that sword. Thyestes then revealed the truth to Aegisthus about how Atreus had killed his half-brother Chrysippos years beforehand. Aegisthus, feeling duty-bound to his long-lost father, killed Atreus, and Mykenai then belonged once more to Thyestes.

Atreus's sons, Menelaos and Agamemnon, took refuge with King Tyndareus of Sparta, meeting his two daughters, Klytemnestra and Helene. After marrying Helene, Menelaos ascended Sparta's throne and aided Agamemnon in overthrowing Thyestes. Agamemnon, who had married Klytemnestra, expanded Mykenai by conquering the surrounding lands and becoming the most powerful man in mainland Hellas.

Agamemnon and Klytemnestra were not besotted with each other but were realists. They understood the gravity of their positions and their responsibilities. They kept their expectations of each other isolated to their duties as a king and queen to build a strong dynasty. As a result, they cooperated well and had a successful marriage. They had three daughters, Iphigenia, Chrysothemis and Elektra, before their son, Orestes, was born. Klytemnestra and Agamemnon loved their daughters. Orestes's long-awaited arrival did not diminish this. Klytemnestra insisted on having a loyal and loving family, so she doted on her daughters and did not exclude them.

From such devotion came great grief when her husband put his sword to Iphigenia in Aulis as a sacrifice to Artemis so the Achaean fleet could sail to Ilion. It should have been no surprise that his ruthless deception of a wedding to Achilleus was faithful to the deceitful nature of his heritage. Having also been fooled by the trick by escorting her daughter to Aulis, Klytemnestra witnessed her unholy death. Ravaged with sorrow and hatred, she swore revenge.

"Lady Hera, Queen of Heaven on Mount Olympos, wife of almighty Zeus, guardian goddess of all wives and women, hear my voice, heed my prayer, and grant me the wisdom and enlightenment that I require," Klytemnestra said under her breath before the altar at my temple in the centre of Mykenai, her arms up and fingers splayed as she knelt, the sacrifice of a cow's liver on my altar.

This woman had prayed to me every day for ten years since the Achaean kings and warriors had left their homeland for the foreign shores to reclaim Helene and sack Ilion, hoping I would answer. Now her husband was due to return; the time was ripe to seize her vengeance.

"Queen Klytemnestra," I said, standing behind her. Her head snapped back to look at me. She stood up from kneeling, leaning one hand on the altar for balance. "My lady Hera," she whispered. "Thank you for answering my call."

"You are the Queen of Mykenai. Your marriage is important."

"Yet, it has failed, my lady. Agamemnon sacrificed my first-born daughter." She choked on her words, her eyes filling with tears. "Alone, I have lived with this anguish all these years. When he returns — whenever that may be — I do not believe I will be able to be the wife I once was. I cannot stand the thought of lying with him, obeying the wishes of the monster who took my precious jewel from me."

Then she grew angry. "I am glad it has been so long since I laid eyes on him. I cannot remember the outline of his face. It would grieve me more to do so. But my daughter's expression as her own father slit her throat? Her bloody clothes, the despair in her eyes, the shock? I can never forget those. So, I have prayed to you because I wish for guidance on how I should act. What does a wife do when her husband kills their daughter?"

I pursed my lips in thought. Truthfully, I was undecided. Yet looking at Klytemnestra's tortured expression as she waited for divine knowledge, I realised what I would do in her situation: what she was planning to do, with or without the gods' blessing.

"If I were you, Klytemnestra, Queen of Mykenai, I would pray to the primordial daughter of Nyx and Erebos, the ancient goddess Nemesis," I told her. "As the lady of retribution, she knows best in times like these."

She looked confused. "You mean I should avenge my daughter?"

"There are three great wrongs which all the gods that have ever been can never forgive. The first is polluting the custom of hospitality, either as a host or guest. The second is regicide: assassinating one's king. The third, and the most heinous, is any blood crime: killing one's own kin."

Klytemnestra narrowed her eyes. "My lady, my husband did not just end my daughter's life. He gave her as a gift to the gods themselves. He was advised to do so by his priest Kalchas."

I shook my head. "The gods do not demand human flesh as a sacrifice. Any reasonably competent priest would know that. At the feast of Mekone, it was decreed that men would offer animal meat to the gods, not their own. Since Zeus is the father of mankind, such an act offends him and all Olympians."

Hope filled the queen's eyes. "Then I am free to act as I wish against my husband?"

I frowned, cautioning her. "If you kill your husband, Haides will treat your soul as he sees fit for a murderer. However, you will not earn the gods' wrath in this life for ridding their world of the one who offended them."

She was struggling to fight down a smile at the idea. I could tell. It was a feeling I had known many times. Then she looked at me earnestly. "As the goddess of marriage, do I have your permission to do this? The last thing I wish is to offend you, my lady."

I thought hard about Zeus' laws. And about mine. What would I do?

"Your piety is a great virtue, Queen Klytemnestra. Truthfully, I would not support the slaying of one's husband, who gives his wife shelter, comfort, food, and protection."

Klytemnestra looked crestfallen. "I see that, my lady."

"However, as the goddess of motherhood, I would send to the depths of Tartaros any man, husband or not, who needlessly took my child's life."

That was when Klytemnestra smiled. It was a wicked, bloodthirsty look. "Thank you, my lady. That is all I needed to hear."

"But do not imagine, Queen Klytemnestra, that your actions will bring you peace or even comfort."

She nodded understandingly. "It is not peace I seek, my lady. I gave up looking for that long ago."

With that, the Queen of Mykenai plotted her revenge and began an affair with Aegisthus, the cousin of Agamemnon.

When Agamemnon returned from Ilion, he brought Kassandra, the Trojan royal priestess of Apollo, as a war captive. The presence of another woman, a Trojan, in her own house enraged Klytemnestra further. She killed her husband with an axe in the bathtub, and Kassandra, too. Both Aegisthus and Klytemnestra took credit for the plot.

Elektra, the youngest daughter of Agamemnon, witnessing the crime and discovering her father's dead body, smuggled her younger brother Orestes out of the palace that night to be reared in safety by a family friend, Pylades. She did this out of concern that once Aegisthus took the throne, he would order Orestes's execution. Many years hence, Orestes returned to the palace as a youth and slew his mother and the usurper, Aegisthus.

Unfortunately, the public reaction to a son murdering his mother was horrifying. There was much debate about whether or not it counted as a blood crime, for many believed a mother's womb was simply a vessel to nurture the seed of the father, nothing more.

To end the generations of bloodshed, Athene set up a council of elected officials in Athens to judge accused murderers, calling it the Areopagus. It was decided that Orestes had not committed a blood crime as he did not share blood with his mother. Apollo, who had spoken on behalf of Orestes, won the day by claiming that Athene, who was presiding, was born from Zeus alone, forgetting Metis.

When I pointed this out to him, Apollo shrugged and said, "Does it matter? A mother still contributes nothing. Ask Father."

Knowing he would agree, I did not go to Zeus. The thought that so many gods believed that a father was solely responsible for the birth of a baby angered me.

You may wonder why I am recounting this story, other than for my small part in counselling Klytemnestra. Put simply, it is essential. Parents devouring children. Cheating, murderous wives. Fathers raping their daughters. Sons killing their mothers. Brothers killing each other. In short, the tales of the House of Atreus tell of possibly the worst family that ever lived. Most of all, the simple lesson is that families fall apart when parents fail to protect their children. I do not know if many have noticed how both the lines of Klytemnestra and Agamemnon shared the lineage of Zeus.

16: AINEIAS

The hero with whom I had the worst strife after the fall of Ilion was one of its princes, a lord called Aineias, a son of Aphrodite, who had been saved by Poseidon on the battlefield of Ilion when Achilleus was about to cut him down. He became one of the first founders of the Roman Empire. According to many, he was the embodiment of piety, which I could not agree with.

The Achaean success at Ilion strengthened my resolve that, as my cause was just and correct, all Trojan princes must be wiped out and that any recreation of Ilion's power had to be stopped, for otherwise, they would likely seek revenge on Mykenai. However, I also knew that Zeus was of the opposite mind, secretly mourning the loss of King Priam's great empire. The quest he ordered Aineias to undertake, to settle the remnants of the Trojan people, was proof of this.

I took much time to debate the decision of whether or not to hinder the course of Aineias and his comrades. I knew that I would struggle to find supporters and that many gods desired peace and were making amends with one another. I knew that if I were to act against Aineias, I would renew my animosity with Aphrodite and possibly create fresh discord with Zeus. It would be no small or insignificant matter to publicly try to thwart his plans and persecute the son of a fellow goddess, especially one as passionate as Aphrodite. But then again, it would not be the first time.

On that fateful night when the city of Ilion was brought to its knees, back down to the foundations laid there centuries before, Prince Aineias fled the carnage with his followers and family, carrying his father, Anchises, on his back while bearing statues of his household gods, the Penates, in one arm and holding the hand of his son Ascanius in the other; this image became the idealised vision of goodness in men for aeons to come — caring for one's father, protecting one's son, and honouring one's gods.

However, Aineias was no better than his cousin, Paris. His adventures to found the city of Rome, the new Ilion, let him reveal his true nature: a barbaric, cowardly, manipulative, treacherous thief.

To start with, while rushing from the burning Ilion, he forgot all about the welfare of his wife, Kreusa. She lagged behind him, carrying the household items they would need, and became lost. She was either slain or burned to death due to her husband's lack of care.

My first action was to visit the guardian of the winds, Aiolos, who lived on the floating island of Aeolia, a place in the sky surrounded by walls of bronze. Only he, save for Poseidon, who was distracted by the wanderings of the King of Ithaka, could completely divert the Trojan's course and hinder their progress. Usually, I would summon a god to my presence. Still, I wished for a private meeting, so I travelled through the sky above the Great Sea towards his shadowy lair, a deep cavern hidden in the mountain depths. Venturing through the craggy rocks, I passed through a dark, dingy tunnel where calcium dripped down the walls. The cold bit at my bare, pale arms. A breeze billowed my dress around me. As I reached the end of the tunnel, I came to Aiolos's throne room, where the god of the winds sat aloft on a great boulder. He had a stocky build, strong arms, an untamed black mane, and a long dark beard.

Aiolos bowed his head. "Queen Hera of Olympos, how may I serve you?"

I smiled at him. "Lord Aiolos, my husband, the King of Heaven, gave you a great responsibility when he took ownership of the sky. He bestowed power over the world's winds, storms, and tempests upon you, dominion over the gales and gusts. You alone can restrain their rage so they do not destroy the world. You ensure the oceans remain calm and let just the right number of leaves fall when autumn is near. There is much to thank you for when speaking of the natural peace of this world."

He seemed pleased at my acknowledgement of his efforts. "I thank you for your kind words, my lady. I take my duties very seriously to preserve the order of the cosmos. I do not let one little breeze out of my grasp. Just glance below your feet, my queen."

So, I did.

Peering over ledge of the rocky path where I stood, I could see the chains and dungeons in which Aiolos kept his tempests. They strained against their shackles with sweat and tears, howling at their master with deep contempt and vain pleading. The strongest of them, the great blasts of the North and South, were incarcerated behind iron bars, prisons built inside the mountain. They did not fly into a frenzy like their brothers and sisters. They waited patiently, calm, before their storms.

Impressed, I looked back at Aiolos. "Then I have come to the right place. A group of Trojan refugees currently sail west to the distant land of Hesperia, a place of wild tribes and no civilisation to speak of, to find a city where they can settle and flourish. Usually, I would have no qualms about such developments, but it is not Hellenic influence which would civilise Hesperia. It would be the barbaric practices of Ilion which would worship false gods, undermining the authority of Olympos."

Aiolos frowned. "Such a thing would indeed be concerning."

"Frightening, I would even say," I corrected him. "Therefore, I command you to release all your winds onto the Great Sea and attack those who are my enemies. Sink them. Scatter them. I do not care what happens to them so long as they are blown off course. Do this well, and I shall give you as a bride one of fourteen Nereides who wait upon me at court, gifted to me as a peace offering from their queen, Thetis. Of these, Deiopea is the most beautiful of them all. She can be yours, being fair company for you here in Aeolia and providing you with many children. Your offspring could form a new clan of nymphs."

He nodded thoughtfully. "My winds would be glad of the freedom. Besides, my dominion would not be mine if Zeus had not been advised to do so after your graceful intercession. Because of you, I am the lord of the winds and am invited to dine with the gods on Olympos. Honour and duty demand I obey your order, my lady, and I shall do so happily."

I smiled, pleased.

With one cast of his staff against the side of the hollow mountain, Aiolos shook the chasm and released the winds from their gaols. They rose from the ground, gathering in their gales, and spilt out of the tunnel entrance to the world outside, zealous to cause chaos. Catching sails and rising almighty waves as high as mountains, they sank many Trojan ships. They drowned many of their sailors and warriors. Frustratingly, Aineias survived. Instead of rushing to save his countrymen or gain control of the vessel, he clung pathetically to his ship's mast. He wept and prayed to the gods above for mercy.

It was the god below who heard him. Poseidon rose from the deep and cast peace over the sea once more, saving Aineias and what remained of his fleet. He then rounded up the scattered winds, admonished them, and sent them home with a reminder to their master that it was not he who had the right to cause the sea to ravage so many souls but his alone.

For six years, I kept Aineias wandering at sea, living on seaweed and from what his men could catch from the water. I might have lost the wind, but I visited enough illness upon them that they became dejected and helpless.

Aineias did not give up. He sailed on to Libya, finally making land. While he was out hunting, he met his mother, Aphrodite, disguised as a huntress. She informed him that nearby lay a growing city called Karthage, built by Phoenician refugees led by their widowed queen, Dido. Fortunately for the lost Trojans, she welcomed strangers to help her people. Aphrodite suggested that the Trojans seek safety there. Glad of the advice, Aineias presented himself before Queen Dido.

The Queen of the Karthaginians was a paragon of widowhood. She had taken her people to a new land south of the Great Sea to find a new kingdom. When her husband, Sychaeus, the wealthiest man in Tyre, had been murdered by her brother, Dido had avenged him and pledged an oath of fidelity to his memory, swearing never to lie with or wed another man again. For this, I greatly admired the mortal queen. I had helped her by showing her the ideal location for her people to build their empire, marked by the head of a horse to signify their future greatness in battle. I was set to make sure Dido would not be friendly to the Trojans.

Aphrodite had other plans. To ensure Aineias received the warmest welcome, she made him appear the most handsome man in the world to the Queen of Karthage. And so, Dido

143

welcomed Aineias and his people to stay for as long as needed. Then Aphrodite instructed her son, Eros, to go to Dido in the shape of Aineias's young son, Ascanius, and enchant her with a spell of love. This Eros did. As Dido cradled the child she thought to be Ascanius, he cast upon her a dreaded curse to forget her pledge to the memory of her late husband and turn her full attention to Aineias.

This greatly annoyed me. First, Poseidon had thwarted my plan. Now Aineias had gained safe entry into the Karthaginian city. I knew Aphrodite did not care that Dido's honour and virtue, even her future, were directly compromised. However, I resolved to make the most of the situation. Matters could still be turned to my advantage. I reasoned the Trojans would, no doubt, seek money and ships for their journey to Hesperia. Still, perhaps Aineias could stay in the perfectly fair city of Karthage, already built by a noblewoman, instead of founding his own city. With this in mind, I went to Aphrodite on Olympos, discovering her braiding her hair on her bed in her bedchamber.

"Queen Hera," she greeted, donning a sickly-sweet smile. "What can I do for you?"

I smiled in return. "I have come to sing your praises, Lady Aphrodite. You and your son, Eros, deserve countless prizes for your achievements in Karthage. What a feat to ensnare the most devout widow into passion and love."

"Oh, thank you," Aphrodite replied, batting her eyelashes. "It was nothing too strenuous for either Eros or me to accomplish. We carry out such infiltrations all the time."

"I wish I had not hunted Aineias in the way I did. I feel terrible. I am tired of bloodshed and sick of suffering. I truly desire peace for all, including your son, Aineias."

She stretched out a smile. "Oh, Hera. It delights me to hear you say such things."

I clapped my hands together. "Then listen, for I have had a splendid thought! Why do we not marry them: Aineias and Dido? Nothing could be more fitting. They can rule together in Karthage. Dido can have her second Tyre, and Aineias can have his second Ilion. What do you say?"

Aphrodite rose to her feet, clasping her hands in front of her, looking sorrowful. She did a great job at her pretence. "I would be a fool to refuse such a happy ending. But we both know that it is Zeus's desire for Aineias to settle in Hesperia. Trust that I have no issue with your suggestion, but if Zeus wishes for the opposite, then it is my lord whom I must obey. Although being his wife, you may be able to sway his mind to the contrary. There are plenty of ways to work your feminine charms on the opposite gender, especially on your husband."

I had no desire to repeat my seduction of Zeus on Mount Ida. At any rate, it was Aphrodite that I needed on my side at the moment.

"I have checked with Zeus. He fully approves," I lied.

She blinked, surprised. "Really? Quite recently, Zeus assured me that the Trojans were bound to reach Hesperia."

"Yet he told me today their destiny lay in Libya," I answered, my cheeks hurting from the strained grin. "My poor husband can't seem to make up his mind, or the Moirai refuse to give a straight answer."

She hesitated, then embraced me tightly. "Then let Dido and Aineias join together with their people. I would love nothing more."

"I shall arrange for it as soon as possible," I assured her, wary of how easily she had agreed to the match. "When Helios goes to the sky next time, the Karthaginians will be joined with the Trojans, and I shall prepare a bridal bed for the pair. You should see your son marry his bride. I shall invite the god of weddings, Hymen. Only then can it be considered a real wedding."

Aphrodite continued smiling and nodded. "Only then."

The Karthaginians and the Trojans rode out the next day to hunt side by side to feed their city. Dido and Aineias, separated from the horde, rode to hunt together. But Helios soon disappeared as the rain was sent down in torrents around them. Rushing to a nearby cave, the two huddled together.

From above, Aphrodite, Hymen and I watched. Hymen spoke the marriage rites as the pair spoke of their golden future, making promises to each other. They fell into each other's arms and consummated their union on the cave floor.

From then on, Dido considered Aineias her husband, as did I. They did everything together. They were in love, I have no doubt. However, as a result of her betrayal of Sychaeus, she could not focus on the prosperity of her kingdom. So the progress of Karthage fell behind. With no order, governance or plan, the people began to do as they wished. The lack of discipline led to disorder. The question of Aineias as king above Dido filled the common folk with resentment, and soon riots broke out.

My instincts and suspicions had been right. Aphrodite and her son were to betray me, as I had feared. Being a child of lust, Aineias was easily corrupted. After being admonished by Hermes, delivering a message from Zeus, he prepared to leave. In their final confrontation, he sank so low as to claim they were never husband and wife since he signed no deal nor had any ceremony before witnesses. *What a fatuous lie!*

Dido was heartbroken. Love's curse had turned against her. Distraught, depressed, and hopeless, she lived her final day when she woke one terrible morning to see the Trojan ships had left the harbour of Karthage for the horizon and Hesperia beyond. Now empty of tears, she turned to her sister, Anna, and ordered for a pyre to be built in the courtyard of her palace, where they were to burn anything that was ever owned by a Trojan. She went to the augurs and read entrails of animals, reading damnation in the remains. That night she proceeded to the pyre when the courtyard was empty. She picked Aineias's sword from the gathered belongings beside the pyre and climbed the pile. Once at the top, gazing out onto the roofs of her city and seeing the Trojan ships in the far distance, she raised her head to the heavens.

I was looking down from the sky upon her in horror.

She opened her mouth and spoke softly into the air. Her voice floated in the wind up to my ears. "Heavenly ones, take my soul. I may be a mortal, but I have also tried to be an honest and hardworking one. I beg you to ease my pain. I wish to go now to the shades below this earth. Trust that I have not lived a forsaken life. I raised a city, punished my traitor brother, and did as the gods commanded. What more could I have done had that treacherous Trojan never come into my home?"

She then leant down and kissed the bed on which she stood, one in which she and Aineias had spent many nights. "Arise an avenger of my blood here in Karthage. Hunt down these hated ones with fire and blades. Let my armies, seas, and lands never meet in harmony with his, and let hate for the Trojan race descend on all in this city."

She seemed to smile, tears falling down her face. "I receive death with pleasure, yearned for many days. It is better now to die than to live. Let the flames of this pyre be a torch whose light the Trojans will see for all their cowardly flight. Let Aineias know well what I have done."

With her final words, she raised the sword, cutting it deep into her heart. Not one scream or anguished sound did she cry. Blood spurted out around her. Her hands became crimson. She collapsed onto the bed, a queen no more as the breath left her body, the blade's sting unyielding. Whatever physical pain she had suffered was nothing compared to that which had inflicted her poor soul, now ready to be relieved of its earthly woes.

Her servants had seen what their monarch had done and rushed out to the courtyard with demented screams and wails, horrified at their queen's suicide.

Dido's sister, Anna, hearing the commotion, exited her room and hurried out to the courtyard. Looking up at the pyre, she saw her dead sister and climbed after her, sobbing, "Was this what you truly asked me to do, Dido? To build your deathbed for you? To not even be there to see you pass?"

She took Dido in her arms. "You have destroyed not just yourself but me, your city and your people, all unfinished and unhappy, with no heir to take the throne. Stay and live. I beg you."

Anna called down to the slaves below. "Bring water! Bring cloth! Bring anything you can lay your hands on."

Then turning back to her sister, she bent her head and kissed her skin. "You can do it. It is not your time yet."

However, Anna was no prophet; as the blood left her sister's body, so would her life.

Knowing it was time, I sent Iris down to fulfil the rites necessary for Haides and Persephone to receive Dido below. Iris cut a lock of hair from the dead queen's head, and Dido's soul was released into the air, her chest releasing a final breath.

Anna released a strangled scream into the air, knowing she was alone. After sobbing into her sister's corpse, she resolved to follow her to the dead below, unable to bear being without her. Anna grabbed Aineias's sword and did as her sister had done.

The Karthaginians had no choice but to burn the pyre that day, now in a funeral.

In the distance, the Trojans saw the flame. I know not what Aineias felt as he watched the beacon of the deaths he had left in his wake, but I hope it was the most profound shame. Dido's end only strengthened my efforts to stop Aineias's ambitions. I sent Iris to the Trojan women to instruct them to burn their husbands' ships when they landed on the island of Sikily. But, once again, my efforts were thwarted.

When the Trojans landed on Hesperia, Aineias went straight to business. He sought the hand in marriage of Lavinia, the daughter of a Latin king aptly named Latinus. However, Lavinia was already betrothed to Turnus, a local chieftain of the Rutulians, who became Aineias's enemy for the competition over Lavinia. And so, once again, a Trojan attempted to steal away the bride of another — this was how I knew Aineias and Paris were one and the same and that the Trojan race was not worthy of life or blessing.

I summoned one of the Erinyes, Alekto, a demon harpy from the Fields of Punishment, to foster hatred of Aineias in the minds of his Latin allies, starting with their queen, a proud and admirable woman called Amata.

After that, I called Alekto up from the deep with a spell. She had large back wings, snakes with long forked tongues for hair, and a malformed, crusted face; a truly heinous creature. When I beheld the malignant spirit of the deep, I was offended.

Nevertheless, I gave her my command: "Maiden of the night, serve me so I might find justice among barbarians. It is in your power to raze realms and upturn kingdoms, to bewitch the most ardent allies into hateful enemies, even those of the same blood. You can bring towns to the torch of death and create ten thousand calamities from a mere thousand. Now, spread jealousy, turmoil, and cruelty from your breast. Do not allow Aineias and the Trojans to deceive the Latins with their false promises of peace when they secretly plan to conquer them. Drive them out of Hesperia. Destroy this false peace which Aineias has forged. Ready all spirits for enmity and all hands for arms."

Alekto's face did not show any sign of emotion or rationality. I doubted she was a creature of reason like most nymphs — those of the Underworld were a different kind entirely, kept away from philosophy and deduction. But I saw a glint in her eye as she realised I had ordered her to torture the living when her sadistic skills had previously been restrained to the dead. Alekto quickly flew off into the dark night of Hesperia, her great wings beating the air like several drums of ships. She then fell upon the door of Queen Amata, who was in her chambers.

Ensuring Alekto would do as I wished, I followed behind, invisible.

I heard Queen Amata in discussion with her husband: the foreigners did not share such views, having landed on their shores and preaching their divine right to invade, a mandate sent from gods she had never heard of. While, at first, they had both been sceptical, it seems Latinus was easily fooled while she had seen through the amiable guise of Aineias. Like most men, he was content his opinion was the right one, and he soon brushed aside her concerns and quickly fell asleep. But the queen was unable to sleep soundly. Her heart had been disturbed by the arrival of the Trojan Aineias seeking her daughter, her pride and joy, the beauty of the kingdom, and who had been so content to marry Turnus, a man much loved in the region and the preferable of the two suitors in her mind; for Turnus was a native who led his people well, viewing the Latins as their equals, even their extended brethren.

Alekto, unseen by mortal eyes, approached Amata's bedside. She climbed over the lady, tossing and turning in her efforts to sleep. Alekto shook out her serpent hair, black and hissing, over Amata. One snake stretched down low enough to fall from the demon's scalp, bite Amata's breast, and sink poison into her flesh and veins, venom for violence and viciousness against her enemies. Then it slithered under her bed linen and crawled over her bare body, leaving venom in its wake and then over her neck, hair, and face before returning to its rightful place in its mistress' palm. Alekto departed from the room, leaving Amata to foster doom.

Amata arose from the bed to find her husband, King Latinus, already dressing for the day. She found it impossible to keep silent, saying: "Do you think this travelling lord shall enjoy our daughter's beds, or will he prefer the lands such sheets would give him?"

Latinus frowned. "What do you mean, woman?"

She clasped his hands in hers. "If you will not pity your daughter, then pity your wife. What will I do when this lord from strange shores leaves this land for another? What would be worse: him leaving Lavinia behind or taking her with her?"

The king shook her off. "We have discussed this. He will do no such thing. You heard him. His destiny lies here."

"Destiny?" she demanded. "Did these Trojans not try to set up their city in Krete, Karthage, and Sikily? Did they not fail in those places when things went awry or when their precious gods told them to move on? Did they not leave the lands in ruin? Did Aineias's own cousin, Paris, not kidnap a Spartan queen who was married, not caring about the war that would ensue? Do not deny it. The whole world knows of Helene of Ilion. We cannot rely upon these Trojans. It would not be wise when Turnus, a man you have known for years, would be your son-in-law, just as you knew his father, a man you trusted. Besides, Lavinia desires a match to Turnus above Aineias. She is good and knows what is suitable for the kingdom's peace. So, to whom shall you give your crown? I know who I would pick. You would die happy if you were to adhere to my words, knowing your descendants will be pure Latins with no trace of eastern blood or preference, descendants who will treasure your memory and traditions. Turn your mind to Turnus, and we shall all be the better for it."

Latinus did not listen to his wife, besotted with the foreign hero as he was, as well as the romantic notion of a nation rebuilt and helping the poor and starving.

Amata raged at her husband, unable to control the temper Alekto had incensed within her. Soon it drove her demented. She ran from the village into the forests, where she defiled the rites of Dionysos, performing them improperly, for she was not in the correct madness for it. Then she sang hymns for the wedding she would never see. Later, she returned home in confusion and sorrow when the spell had lifted. From then on, she took to her room and would see no one.

Meanwhile, Aineias and Turnus's feud had grown, with the Latins trying to remain neutral. At this, Zeus called a council of the gods to settle the matter. He allowed Aphrodite and I to each make a speech before the Olympian court in favour of our personal cause.

Aphrodite went first: "Oh, great gods of Olympos, to whom else can I turn for support? Gaze upon the haughty Rutulians of Hesperia; how they, audaciously and without impunity, insult my son who came to them for aid; how arrogant Turnus makes a spectacle of himself; and how this has brought bloodshed. My son, Aineias, remains in danger. Yet his destiny, handed to him by Zeus, is to rediscover the lost Ilion. The lands of Latinus are his by divine right, yet now I fear for his life. We need your help, your aid, and your allegiance. Refuse, and you denounce the will of the King of Heaven, like his own wife, who has sought to frustrate my son's attempts to obey the gods at every turn, only causing further damage; Aiolos, Iris, Alekto, to name but a few who have aided her foolish, vain desires."

I surged up from my seat, unwilling to listen to this slander. "Is that what you think of me? One who has no will of her own? What a hypocrite you are. You forget the Trojans are thieves and tricksters. What right does Aineias possess to terrorise the peaceful people of Hesperia when your bloodline belongs to Kyprus? It is there he should seek, if anywhere at all, to start his damned city, doomed to fall, just like Pergamum itself. Shall you ignore his selfish cowardice in deceiving Dido, letting her die? Besides, you cannot rightly say who has given him his divine mandate. Was it the Moirai, Zeus, Apollo, Iris, you or I who steered him on? Whoever it may be, they also wove in my fate with his. You cannot lay the blame for his demise at my feet alone when I am led by a higher power, just like you. But why am I attempting to reason with the epitome of irrational lust? You slander me publicly because you fear my victory. Unfortunately, your calls for aid come too late. Turnus already has the country on his side, ready to defend it against your lecherous offshoot and his pack of pirates."

Zeus rose from his throne. "Both of you, cease this now. I can assure you that the Trojans and the Latins are all the same to me. From now on, the Moirai will be the only ones to influence the fate of either race."

At his words, the heavenly ones bent their heads, agreeing to put an end to this summit. As I caught her gaze, I knew that Aphrodite would not be so easily swayed to give up her side of the fight, as neither would I.

I don't know how she did it, but Aphrodite convinced Hephaistos, her ex-husband, to make Aineias a shield, another blow to my confidence. When the Latins, in alliance with the Trojans, met on the battlefield of their ultimate clash, Turnus challenged Aineias to single combat for the kingdom and the hand of Lavinia. Aineias, agreeing, promised that whoever won would take Lavinia's hand and rule in equity with the Latins, with Latinus as their king.

I feared for Turnus's welfare. First, conjuring up a vision of Aineias, I attempted to lure Turnus away from his battle to the ships. However, this only drove him to question his value as a warrior, and he nearly took his own life. So, I let him return to the battlefield.

Then I summoned his sister Juturna, a lake nymph, telling her to mind her brother's back, saying: "Nymph Juturna, though we have not met before, you are very dear to me, for I side with your brother, Turnus, that champion of the Rutulians, who have fought well and have been protected by me, but now who meets his destiny. I cannot bear the thought, never mind seeing such horror as could befall him soon, going to meet Aineias man-on-man, for I fear the Trojan, the better of the two."

"You do not really think this shall happen, do you? That my brother will perish on the battlefield today?" she asked, her brow knitted in concern.

"Fret not. If you do as I say, such a thing should not happen. Hurry and help your brother by whatever means you can. Urge the men to fight by his side, for we shall have a better chance of success. Go now, with my blessing, and do as I command for your brother's sake and the good of this land."

Juturna, donning abandoned armour and appearing before the Latin army as one of their noble soldiers, convinced them to break the treaty, taking advantage of the natives' animosity toward the invaders. Then when one Latin youth cast a spear at the opposing side, an ungodly struggle broke out between the two sides.

Aineias shouted out for his men to stop but to no avail, receiving an arrow in the knee for which he had to retreat from the battlefield. When the physician failed to remove it safely, Aphrodite cured her son. At the same time, Turnus laid waste to the Trojan troops outside. Undeterred, Aineias rose from his bed and gathered his men, attacking Latinus's city, where Amata hanged herself upon seeing the assault on her walls. Turnus followed Aineias to the town and challenged him to a duel to end the war. Aineias met him in the courtyard, and the last fight began. First, they hurled their spears. Then they clashed swords. Turnus dropped his and shouted for a new one. Juturna tossed him one. The two men fought once more with blood, sweat, iron, tears, and courage abounding.

Looking down at the action from above, Zeus appeared at my side.

"You realise it is fruitless when the Latins are fated to fall to the Trojans," he began, speaking calmly.

"This may not be, my lord." I closed my eyes.

"Do you argue with my opinion, which is fact and not fable?"

"No, my lord."

"Then you simply wish to ignore it and try your luck," he continued. "In doing so, you will destroy the lives and livelihoods of thousands of Latins. Aineias will bring no harm to them once they swear allegiance to him."

I cast my eyes to the ground, sorrowful. I could feel the impending defeat. "Then Turnus must die, even though he is the rightful husband of Lavinia?"

He nodded. "As an enemy leader, he must die, although I would not say he is her rightful husband. They may have been promised to each other and may have loved each other, but that does not constitute a marriage. This you must know of all beings."

I hesitated and then nodded. Although I hated to admit it, Zeus was right.

"Give up the fight," he advised. "All you do is delay the inevitable and prolong the suffering of the poor souls. Is it not time that peace was finally settled throughout this world? Let what will be, be. Besides, is Aineias truly your enemy?"

With those words, my husband ended my hunt for Aineias.

I stared at Zeus, finally seeing that from the start, from the day I went to war, my strength and efforts had been misplaced. No, Aineias was not my enemy, I realised, looking at my husband, who wasn't looking back at me. He wasn't even close.

Casting my gaze on the fight, I resolved to let Turnus die.

Whether or not I agreed, Zeus hastened Turnus's demise, sending down an Eiryne to frighten Turnus and distract him. Aineias, using his advantage, cast his spear and hit Turnus's leg. The Rutulian begged for mercy. Aineias might have shown him clemency, but remembering the Trojan lives lost to the Latins, he killed his foe, driving a sword into his breast and sending Turnus to the Underworld.

The last I saw of Aineias was when he took Princess Lavinia of the Latins to bed. I pitied the poor young woman just as I pitied the dead Turnus. I pitied the people of Hesperia, who would now be subject to the rule of imperialist foreigners who would establish the settlement of Lavinium, named after Aineias's bride.

Ascanius would inherit his father's throne one day, moving the city to Alba Longa. Later, two sons, fathered by Ares, would be born to the priestess Rhea Silva, who was then cast into a river and executed as she, a Vestal Virgin, had broken her sacred vow of chastity. The babies, Romulus and Remus, were rescued and suckled by a she-wolf, some say a prostitute, for the words in Latin are the same, and raised by a shepherd. When they grew up, they founded the city of Rome, which would, in the coming years, conquer all around it, starting with the Latins. Their empire stretched from Aegyptos and Lybia in the south to Kaledonia in the north and Armenia in the east.

As for me, I never stopped hating the Trojans and, after them, their Roman race. They enslaved Hellas and created fake versions of the Olympian gods. My counterpart was Juno. No, try as I might, I never stopped being disgusted by the descendants of Aineias.

However, I had learnt something important: I only had one true enemy. Spending my strength to harm anyone else was a waste.

17: TIRESIAS

The Olympian gods were beginning to reconcile their differences, move on from the war, and return to their lives. The same happened with my marriage. Nothing would ever change between Zeus and me. I came more firmly to this conclusion when I met Tiresias, whom Zeus had invited to Olympos shortly after the Trojan War. He was reportedly a traveller and a wise man, not that I have ever agreed with such accounts.

"Hera!" Zeus called out, waving his hand at me. "Come here."

I had been pacing alone in the sunny courtyard, reflecting on the war. However, I obliged him and moved towards the archway. There, I saw my husband was not sitting alone. I glimpsed him on the other side of the archway, in the dining hall.

On his left sat an older man whom I had never seen before. He had a scraggly beard clogged with stray bits of cooked bird skin and grease as he bit into a chicken thigh. The hairs were purpled by the goblet of wine he clutched in his other hand.

I approached them and curtseyed slightly in Zeus's direction.

The older man bowed his head at me.

"This is my guest, Tiresias," my husband said, gesturing to the stranger. "A famous soothsayer and priest of Apollo from Thebes."

Tiresias gave me a toothy grin, yellow and wide.

I tried to return the smile but found myself grimacing instead.

"A remarkable man," Zeus praised, clapping him on the back. "He spent seven years as a woman."

I blinked at the soothsayer in surprise. "Indeed, that is a wonder. A miracle, even, one might think."

"Indeed, it was, my lady," Tiresias replied, chuckling. "For it was you who did it to me." He jabbed a finger at me, narrowing his eyes.

"Excuse me?" I asked, taken aback and unsure if it was an accusation. "I am afraid I do not recall."

"Oh, I understand that you, the Queen of Heaven, cannot possibly be expected to remember all your victims," he said. "Not to worry. When I was like you, I became one of your priestesses, married and had a family. It was not that bad. Then you changed me back." He sent me a reassuring wink.

I forced a smile. "Remind me why I decided to give you such a fate."

"He struck a pair of snakes that were having some … alone time," Zeus explained.

He shared a grin with Tiresias, who raised his eyebrows knowingly. "And so, you cursed him to be a woman. Then, seven years later, he found another pair of similarly compromised snakes but left those to their business and was freed from his curse."

He turned to Tiresias. "Now you know not to interfere with the marriage chamber, even those of animals."

Tiresias bowed his head. "Yes, my lord," he agreed with a light chuckle.

Upon reflection, it did sound like something I would do.

"Did you enjoy being a woman?" I asked him, clasping my hands in front of me.

Tiresias hummed slightly, his eyes searching the air. "It was not that bad. Women are always moaning about their lot, but I found their way of life quite tolerable and pleasant."

I tried not to be disappointed or annoyed with his answer, but I failed.

"Your life, was it a curse? Living in seclusion, having a husband and children?" I asked.

"Yes, tell me," Zeus interrupted before Tiresias could answer, "how was the sex? You know, as a woman? What was it like?"

I felt my cheeks go hot. *To bring up such a subject in front of me!*

Tiresias's eyes widened, blinking. "Oh, that is difficult to answer, my lord."

"Wait, do not tell me. Let us have a bet!" Zeus declared, turning to me. "What is your opinion, Hera? Who has more pleasure in bed: a man or a woman?"

I stared back at him in mute shock. I confess I was offended by the question, not because it was such a lewd topic but because of the position that it put me in. Did he expect me to answer that? How should I know? I took in his face: excited with a glint of mischief in his eyes, utterly ignorant of the effect this entire conversation, not to mention this stupid bet, was having on me.

"Men," I heard myself say without much hesitation.

Zeus clapped his hands, looking back at his guest. "My wife chooses men. Well, I think women have a better time in bed. Well, certainly every woman I have met."

The two burst into howling laughter.

I was appalled, mortified, and offended.

After they settled down, Tiresias said, "As it happens, my lord, my lady, the answer is a complicated one. I shall not lie. I have found that men can often be satisfied more easily,

160

therefore more quickly. On the other hand, I will admit that a woman's pleasure, even though it is more difficult to achieve, is stronger in its sensation. However, the experiences are different."

"Yet men are pleasured more often and with more ease?" Zeus asked.

Tiresias nodded.

My husband clapped his hands again in victory. "I shall take that as a victory. No hard feelings, dear?" he asked me, laughing.

Women had more pleasure, did they? It made me furious that I could not agree and did not know.

My hand lashed out, flinging a spell at Zeus. I had not even thought about what I was doing until it happened. It was simply a reflex.

Eyes widening, Zeus dodged it, and the enchantment smacked Tiresias in the face.

Flung from his dining chair, our guest toppled to the ground. He howled in pain. His hands shot to his face, red blood spurting from his eye sockets.

"Hera!" Zeus exclaimed, kneeling next to the wriggling, wailing Tiresias. "You've blinded him," he scolded, giving me a disapproving look. "This man is our guest."

Clenching my jaw, further enraged that I had missed my target, I swept away from the scene, wishing I had never entered it in the first place.

I was punished, of course, for breaking the custom of hospitality and harming a guest. I was made to care for Tiresias until his eyes healed and he had learned to live as a blind man. For Tiresias's pains, Zeus gifted him the skill of prophecy.

Meanwhile, Zeus publicly condemned my actions, claiming in front of the royal court that they were thoughtless and hysterical. He reassured everyone that they were perfectly safe in the Olympian palace and that guests were always welcome and cared for under his roof. Zeus did not dole out any further humiliation or pain, at least none that he was aware of. He didn't care how everyone in the court treated me; only those who had to be in my presence were. He didn't seem to notice that even some of my own family avoided me.

For the first time, I felt like I fully understood him. Zeus was not even upset that Tiresias had been maimed for life under his watch. He was not ashamed of me or disappointed in me. He didn't stop the calls for exile and slavery as due punishment, nor did he try to stop the bitterness and hate bred by such talk. He just wanted to ensure the blame was not on him. That was the point. Marriage, my role, my institution, and my identity meant nothing to him. However, in this, I also recognised that understanding one's enemy was the first step to defeating him. This realisation ultimately led me to achieve the retribution I sought and thought I deserved.

However, it was not the last I would hear of Tiresias.

18: OIDIPOUS

The Heroic Age was not at an end just yet, despite the fall of Ilion. Elsewhere in the world, great evils and great men were willing to defeat them. One such place was Thebes.

Once upon a time, Zeus seduced a pretty young princess called Antiope, taking the form of a satyr, and impregnated her. In shame, she fled her home while her humiliated father killed himself. Antiope was pursued by her uncle, the regent of Thebes, to come home. Captured, she gave birth on her return to twin boys, Amphion and Zethus. However they were abandoned and raised by others, while Antiope was enslaved and tortured for years by her aunt. However, her persecution did not diminish her spirit. In time, she fled and learned her sons were alive. Upon finding them, they agreed to avenge her years of torment. They killed her uncle and tied his aunt to the horns of a bull that ripped her apart. Then, they built the walls of Thebes around Kadmos's citadel, called the Kadmeia.

At this time, Kadmos's descendant Laios inherited the throne but was too young to rule. And so, Amphion and Zethus usurped the throne. For his safety, Laios was smuggled out of the city and fled to Pisa, ruled by Pelops, the son of Tantalos. Later on, Laios reclaimed the empty throne since Amphion and Zethus had both since perished.

Despite his inclinations, Laios married Iokaste, another descendant of Kadmos, for Laios knew the royal dynasty needed an heir to the throne. Alas, Laios received a prophecy from the Oracle of Delphi that his child would one day be his killer and would marry his wife. Laios then avoided his wife's bed at all costs.

However, one evening, wine made him forget this. He clambered into Iokaste's bed and fathered Oidipous. In the morning, he swore to take away any child born of the union. The newborn baby was exposed on Mount Kithaeron with stakes put through his feet, earning him the nickname Oidipous, 'swollen foot'.

A shepherd rescued the boy, and ultimately, he ended up in the royal nursery of the King and Queen of Korinth, Polybus and Merope, many leagues away. Oidipous had a fine upbringing in Korinth, which was, like much of the rest of Hellas, a vibrant city full of warriors, merchants, brothels, and philosophers — everything a young man needed to become a well-rounded individual in those days. There was much to be enjoyed about life there, the only hindrance to his enjoyment being the wounds in his feet which never completely closed.

His pleasant life in Korinth was not to last, though, as the Moirai had other plans for young Oidipous. One night, at a brothel, he heard from one of his drunken companions that he was not the genuine offspring of the King and Queen of Korinth. Determined to prove this wrong or discover the truth, he visited the Oracle of Delphi, who informed him of the prophecy it had delivered to Laios many years prior — that Oidipous would kill his father and marry his mother. Horrified by this, Oidipous left Korinth without so much as a farewell to those he thought his parents.

His travels brought him to Thebes, guarded by the great Sphinx, whom, long ago, I had inflicted upon the city for their crimes in accepting Kadmos as their king, who had publicly humiliated me at his wedding when he divulged the affair of his sister, Europa, with Zeus. The Sphinx was a great monster with a woman's head, the body of a lioness, and a great set of bird wings. She had vicious claws, ready to pounce upon travellers. While she remained, the city could not access the outside world, making it harder to thrive.

However, she was not a monster without reason. All travellers could turn away, journey elsewhere, and live safely. If one should proceed, one had to accept her challenge and answer a riddle. If one answered incorrectly, one would, of course, be eaten. If one answered correctly, one was allowed free passage to the city.

It was an odd citizenship test, but the Thebans, like many of their fellow Hellens, had an affinity for intelligence. In time, despite her threatening presence, they reasoned that if one was smart enough to discover the answer to her riddle, one was smart enough to live in their society. Nevertheless, many hoped for one intelligent enough to outwit her and strong enough to kill her.

That day, Oidipous was either arrogant or desperate, for he agreed to answer her riddle and risk death. The riddle went as follows: "What walks on four legs in the morning, two in the afternoon, and three in the evening?"

The Sphinx must have licked her lips in hungry anticipation as she gazed at Oidipous, who rubbed his wispy chin.

However, quick as could be, he answered: "A man."

"What?" she said. "Are you sure that you do not want to think about it?"

Apparently, he shook his head and grinned. "The answer is a man. He walks on four legs as a toddler at the start of his life, two legs as an adult for most of his life but then uses a cane in his old age at the end of his life."

The Sphinx was one of those proud creatures that did not take kindly to meeting her match. It seems, in her despair, she threw herself down the mountain to her death.

Oidipous continued until he came to a crossroads where a chariot stopped before him, driven by a slave, transporting his master. However, when the nobleman ordered him to move out of the way, Oidipous refused, stating he had been there first. Their argument turned into a brawl, and Oidipous killed him. The fortunate slave managed to escape.

Not thinking much of this, Oidipous finally reached Thebes, where it was announced that the king had been killed, attacked on the road leading out of the city. The queen, although a descendent of Kadmos in her own right, could not rule, so she needed a new husband to keep the peace.

Oidipous, not the humble type as with any hero, recognised as a stranger to the city, toured the taverns regaling all on how he had vanquished the Sphinx. All who heard it were impressed, not least Queen Iokaste. It was decreed such intelligence would be a great addition to the Kadmian line. Thus, it came to pass that Oidipous married his mother.

I was disgusted. As I supervised their wedding ceremony that night, I had to fight down the bile in my throat. I couldn't even watch. I just listened, and it brought up memories. But the couple did not know their blood connection.

Almost as soon as they were wed, a plague struck the city of Thebes. It was clear to the mortals that the gods were angry with them for some reason. It lasted long enough for the royal pair to have four children: Polynikes, Eteokles, Antigone, and Ismene.

Determined to resolve the plague, King Oidipous sent Kreon, Iokaste's brother, to the Oracle at Delphi. Kreon returned and told Oidipous that the murderer of King Laios must be found, tried and brought to justice, and only then would the plague end. Oidipous vowed to exile the killer of his wife's late husband and sought suggestions for how to do this since many years had passed. Kreon then proposed that they seek the skilled prophet called Tiresias, who was now blind.

Summoned to Thebes, Tiresias, knowing the truth, advised Oidipous not to search for the killer of Laios. However, Oidipous was frustrated, under pressure from the people to end the plague. He declared that the old man did not have any intelligence at all, much less wisdom. Not caring to be insulted by the king, Tiresias announced that Oidipous himself had murdered Laios.

It was as if time stood still, but only briefly, before Oidipous unleashed his fury, claiming this was a ruse. The raised voices carried to Iokaste's room. Soon she was before the court, recalling how Laios had been killed.

Suddenly, a messenger came from Korinth: King Polybus had died.

Oidipous was relieved, for it meant he was not responsible for his father's death. Afraid of what might follow, for he remembered the second part of the prophecy, he asked the messenger to send his condolences to his mother — such was the plague he could not go himself to Korinth to comfort her, fearing he would somehow end up marrying her. However, the messenger reassured Oidipous that he was, in fact, adopted, so he need not feel any pressure to go himself.

Upon hearing this, Iokaste fled the room, realising the terrible truth.

Oidipous could not believe what was happening. He ordered the shepherd that had saved him as a young baby to be found. With this, it did not take long to learn the truth and see his destiny had been fulfilled. Going to Iokaste, he found her dead in her bedchamber, having hanged herself.

Distraught and ashamed, he tore the brooch from her gown and stuck the pin into each of his eyes, blinding himself. In agony, he got down on his knees and prayed for the wisdom of Tiresias and went into exile.

In his absence, Oidipous's two sons, Eteokles and Polynikes, arranged to share the kingdom, each taking an alternating one-year reign. However, Eteokles refused to cede his throne after his year as king. Polynikes summoned an army to oust him from his position, and a battle ensued. At the end of the fight, the brothers killed each other, after which Iokaste's brother, Kreon, took the throne.

Kreon decided that Polynikes had been a traitor and should not receive proper funeral rites. In the act of sacrilege, his body was left unburied to be feasted on by birds and dogs, so his soul could not pass into the Underworld. Defying this edict, claiming that the gods' rule was consistently more potent than that of men, Antigone, the elder daughter of Oidipous, attempted to bury her brother.

Discovering her disobedience, Kreon buried her alive in a tomb, after which she hanged herself like her mother. Haemon, her betrothed and Kreon's son, killed himself when he discovered her body. As a result, Kreon's wife did the same. And so, Kreon's punishment was to live alone in misery, for Ismene, Antigone's sister, left Thebes in search of her long-lost father, Oidipous.

Such was ruination of the curse of incest, as Gaia told me long ago.

19: ODYSSEUS

As Agamemnon and Menelaos were making their different ways home from Ilion, so were the other victors. But unlike the rest of the warriors who had left, it would take Odysseus, the king of the island realm of Ithaka, and his men a further decade to sail home.

Ilion had been a technical challenge for the Achaean military. Odysseus was the visionary of the wooden horse. His genius had won the war, so regard was unmatched in the eyes of many. So when he was absent from leaders' summits the year after the war, anxiety grew about his whereabouts, what had happened to him and if he was still alive or dead. And what, they wondered, did this mean for his kingdom on the far west of Hellas?

In his absence, his son Prince Telemachos, who was little more than twenty years old, and guided by his mother, Queen Penelope, acted as regent, but, with no sign of Odysseus, suitors started to arrive at the palace more regularly. Soon the queen was being harassed by over one hundred suitors who gathered at the court to win her hand, leaving Prince Telemachos obliged to politely host all these men who wanted to disinherit him. As the years went on, it grew increasingly difficult to manage the persistent interest of these men and their various fractious retinues. Telemachos and his mother became exhausted, and it started to drain the kingdom's finances.

Penelope prayed to me for guidance in her wisdom, not knowing what to do against these men with her husband absent. I decided to help her, impressed by her devotion to

Odysseus, who she did not know was alive or dead. Odysseus had shown his foresight in giving up a chance to win Helene's hand all those years ago because, in Penelope, he had found the wisest woman of her generation, who challenged him and proved herself to be more than his equal when it came to problem-solving and challenges of the mind. I had previously only seen her dedication to him in Dido, who had sworn to remain loyal to her late husband's memory. Still, this time, I refused to let Penelope go astray.

I inspired her to promise the suitors that, after accepting her husband would never return, she would choose one of them once she had finished weaving his funeral shroud. This took her three years, for, at night, she unravelled what she had woven throughout the day. The trick was supposed to last as long as needed. Still, her maidservant betrayed her secret, and the suitors once more demanded Penelope make up her mind.

Odysseus, too, was keen to return to his wife. Yes, he had been reluctant to go to the war, and had used his ingenuity to aid victory, and may even have pursued sexual outlets at Ilion — after all, he was a long time away from his wife — but it was Penelope who occupied his mind for all those years of absence; when he lay alone in bed he wondered what Penelope would say about it if she were at his side.

On the score of his marriage, Odysseus was more admirable than most. He appreciated his wife for her mind and spirit; where her intelligence would have been vilified by other husbands, it was not by Odysseus. He saw what I had spent my entire life trying to get Zeus to see. It was that same intellect which ultimately brought him home.

First, he and his men had ended up on the island of the Lotus-Eaters, who made them forget about going home to Ithaka. Then they landed on the island of the one-eyed

Kyklopes, where they were trapped by King Polyphemos, the son of Poseidon, in a cave. Odysseus used his wits to blind him before smuggling his men out of captivity. Then the god of the winds, Aiolos, gave Odysseus a bag containing all the winds that would help take him home. Still, as they neared the shores of Ithaka, his men opened the bag out of curiosity, and the winds blew them back the way they had come. They returned to Aiolos for aid again, but he refused once the god knew Odysseus had angered Poseidon by harming his son.

After the Laestrygonians, a tribe of cannibalistic Gigantes, destroyed most of their ships, they encountered the Titan sorceress Kirke who turned Odysseus's men into pigs. Odysseus escaped her spell by drinking a protective potion. Kirke, having fallen in love with his intelligence, freed his men. She was possibly the closest to permanently parting Odysseus from his wife in his heart, for her skill and ingenuity were divine. He spent a year with her, but his men persuaded him to return home, after which he came across the ghost of the deceased blind prophet Tiresias in the Underworld, who informed him to consult the Sibyl for further guidance on how to get home. Afterwards, they bypassed the Sirens, whom Demeter had cursed years ago when they refused to help her find her missing daughter. Then they suffered some casualties after coming across the monsters Scylla and Charybdis. Then they landed on the island of Thrinakia, where Odysseus's men hunted and killed the cattle of Helios.

In punishment for this crime, Helios sent Odysseus to the island of Ogygia. Even in the Age of Heroes, this place was considered a mythical location. A Titaness called Kalypso, who lived there alone, fell in love with him. For several years, she tried to get him to stay with her forever, however, he refused, trying to find ways to escape. At last, Athene went to Zeus and requested he intervene to send Odysseus home. Zeus sent Hermes to do this, telling Kalypso she had to let him go. Reluctantly the Titaness agreed and helped Odysseus build a raft upon which he could find his homeland again.

Once back in the sea, Poseidon destroyed his vessel. The hero washed up on the shores of Scherie, where Princess Nausikaa of the Phaeacians took him back to the palace. Her parents hosted him and listened to his tales of how he had been thrown over the whole of the Great Sea by Poseidon, who hated him after blinding Polyphemos. They were so impressed with his tale that they returned him home to Ithaka while he slept. He woke up and received the help of Athene in disguise, who informed him of the situation at the palace, still being overrun with suitors running out of patience for Queen Penelope; now it was known she had been scheming to never finish his funeral shroud. Meanwhile, Telemachos had just returned after leaving the island searching for his father.

In disguise, Odysseus went to the palace as a suitor. He briefly met his dog Argos, aged and decrepit, lying in a pile of his dung, uncared for and unloved. However, Argos recognised his master, despite his appearance. After wagging his tail, Argos lost the last of his strength and passed away before him.

After wiping away his tears, Odysseus entered the palace, where he met his wife, Penelope. She, hearing he had news of her husband, interrogated him. Then when he was finally allowed to stay, the housekeeper, Eurykleia, recognised him but was sworn to silence.

Penelope was then inspired to make the suitors compete for her hand, and Odysseus took part: she would wed whoever was strong enough to shoot the king's bow with the most ease through twelve axes. Odysseus succeeded and was declared the winner, after which he discarded his disguise and slaughtered the suitors with his son's help — Telemachos hanged several servants who reportedly betrayed the house for the suitors' causes.

However, Penelope remained wary of Odysseus after being apart from him for twenty years. She instead deceived her husband into telling him something only he would know: their marriage bed was immovable, stuck to the floor by being built into a tree. Overwhelmed with joy, the married couple embraced, and Odysseus reclaimed his rightful place as ruler of Ithaka with a loyal and loving wife at his side.

I envied Penelope greatly, and wondered what it had taken to bring her such a man who was so loyal and devoted to her in his mind and spirit. Unfortunately, although I eventually found love, it would never be in my marriage with Zeus. This thought brought me lower than I had ever been before.

20: KYDIPPE

I heard a whisper in my ears. It awakened me from my dreams: a woman's voice. For a brief, alarming moment, I thought it might be Echo returning to haunt me again. However, I realised I did not know this voice calling me to come to her aid.

Glancing around me, the place quiet, I knew I had nothing better to do with my time than tend to her. I needed something to make me feel better, and it would be refreshing to be with someone who wanted me.

I left Olympos, following the invocation carried on the winds. I fell through the air, knowing I would land exactly where I was required. My feet met with the ground of Delphi.

As the sun beat down on the city, I saw a festival procession. Men and women were revelling in the streets, all wearing garlands, heading towards my temple, loudly beating drums and blowing horns.

In disguise, I followed the crowd as I took in the building. It was tall and authoritarian while retaining an elegance of structure with white marble columns and new steps leading up to the entrance of double doors, through which I would, no doubt, see a statue of my likeness.

Suddenly the crowd became confused. Turning around to the sound of alarmed cries, a cart interrupted the festivities, pushing past people and knocking some aside. It carried a woman dressed like one from my priesthood, moving towards me. The cart was not pulled by oxen but by two exhausted young men. After stopping and staring around them and then at each other, they collapsed to the ground, startling the onlookers. By now, they were barely panting for breath and seemed too weak to move.

Crying in despair, the woman jumped from the cart and rushed to the boys, touching their faces with worry and calling out for aid.

Approaching them, I addressed her. "Priestess, who are these youths to you?"

She looked at me, distraught.

"My sons," she replied, her voice trembling. "When the oxen were not delivered to our door, they carried this cart forty-five stadia to bring me to this festival in honour of my lady, Queen Hera, the goddess I serve. They showed such devotion that I prayed to the goddess for their best blessings, but not this. Please, not this."

She sobbed into the hair of one of them, clutching onto the blistered hand of the other.

I kneeled next to her. "What are their names?" I asked gently.

She glanced at me. "Kleobis and Biton."

Reaching out my hands, I touched each of them lightly on their cheeks, murmuring under my breath.

"What are you doing?" she demanded.

I removed my hands — the spell was complete.

"Hey!" she yelled, pushing me aside. "Who are you?"

I looked at her in alarm. "I am Queen Hera of Olympos."

The spectators gasped in astonishment.

Eyes widening, she bowed her head. "Forgive me," she said quietly, her face pale. "I am humbled. I did not mean to dishonour you, my lady."

"What is your name?" I asked, getting to my feet and brushing down my skirts.

"Kydippe."

"Forget my festival, Priestess Kydippe, and see after your sons," I replied. "As a mother, I can sympathise with your plight. On this day, you will receive no penalty for your negligence of my temple."

"Will they live?"

I shook my head. "I am afraid not. They are already dead."

Her body grew still, and her chest moved in quick breaths. She looked at her sons in devastation and held her hands to their mouths to feel the breath I had just deprived them of.

"No!" she cried out. "What has happened? What have you done?"

She glanced at me, teary-eyed. "My treasures. I do not understand. I wanted them to live."

The crowd was still and silent.

"Life is not as good as it seems," I told her. "Women bleed to death on the birthing bed or from the pain between their legs. Children perish in their mother's wombs or when the cold of the world hits their skin, too weak to survive. Men kill each other daily. Some think they're lucky to survive maimed. Suppose you are wealthy enough to own a house and some land; you will be scrutinised by others who have the same, thrust into a world of survival for superiority. If you survive but have no sons to take care of you, you are thrown out into the street, forced to sell your body or steal to eat. Life is no better for those born into poverty or the slaves beaten or raped. Once you have something to lose, everyone wishes for you to lose it, and it becomes even more of a struggle to enjoy and keep it."

She looked at me appalled, waiting for my words of consolation.

I raised an eyebrow. "You prayed for the highest blessing. That is what they have. Your boys will be happier with my

176

brother Haides in the Fields of Asphodel, where at least the only thing to mourn or worry over is an eternity of dullness. And suppose they were as excellent as you say. In that case, they may even reach Elysian Fields where they will live in blessed contentment, mingling with the greatest minds of history and dancing for the rest of time, with all the pleasures they could ever ask for. Is that not better?"

She did not seem to hear me, lying down in the mudded street, pulling her boys into her embrace and wailing shamelessly, her cries launching into the sky.

The crowd stared after me as I turned away, before I grew too yearnful for their fate.

Yes, there was nothing I wanted more than to die. What I would have given at that moment to be mortal. What I would not have sacrificed to surrender my immortality. Who I would not have betrayed or neglected or killed to be allowed a safe, peaceful, eternal place in the kingdom of my brother, Haides. Even if he sent me straight to Tartaros, at least there I knew I would live with monsters I would understand.

As I walked away, I thought of this beautiful world of nature and sunlight and the horrors held in every corner, including me. I had become one. Although I judged all around me, I had assumed my own perfection, yet had a list of crimes long enough to make Priapos blush. I had hurt, betrayed, mistreated, and abused almost as much as my husband had, if not more. I had given up love for hate. In my search for respect and freedom, I had only invited more nemeses and cages.

Lying awake at night, unable to sleep due to the screams and the dreams, I only had my own dark, depressed, distressed, demented ideas for solace. What I would not give to be able to leave it all behind. However, I had tried everything. Still, I had failed. My fall from grace had been slow and unclear to most at first, but I had kept falling, and now I was at the bottom, but not yet low enough. I wanted to sink deeper into oblivion.

After being in Heaven, Hell would be so much better.

21: IXION

Walking through the doors into the entrance hall, with my diadem in my hands, I saw that the entire marble hall was empty save for one man. I halted, knowing he was a stranger, even with his back to me. I cleared my throat loudly.

He turned to face me. I admit his appearance caught me off guard. Although not as towering as Zeus, he was tall, well-built, and had broad shoulders. It was as if he had been battered by the elements, dressed in a dirty tunic, worn sandals and a torn cloak. His skin was tanned from a life spent outdoors. His cheeks were slightly flushed below a mass of brown hair. However, it was his eyes that were the most captivating. They twinkled like a royal blue night sky.

He approached me with an honest, hopeful smile and a hand on his chest. "Oh, good day, madam. I am King Ixion of the Lapiths, the most ancient tribe of Thessaly."

I frowned. "You do not look like a king."

He glanced down at himself. "Forgive my appearance. I used to be." He chuckled drily.

"What is that supposed to mean?"

His smile faded. "I am an exile. It is a long story."

"I have all the time in the world," I retorted.

He blinked, seeming taken aback.

I caught myself and sighed. "Forgive me. You find me not in the best of moods. Tell me, why have I found you here?"

"I come at the invitation of the almighty Zeus, King of the Olympians. But it seems no one is here to welcome me."

"Well, I am now." I realised he had no idea who I was, and so I donned my diadem. "I am Queen Hera."

His eyes widened, and he stepped back, sweeping a low bow. "Queen Hera, forgive me. I did not —"

"Do not apologise," I interrupted him. "It was refreshing not to be recognised for once. Please, rise."

He straightened up.

"How long will you be at Mount Olympos? I am your hostess. I must know what to prepare for your stay."

He smiled. "Zeus promised me hospitality, that is all. I do not know how long he means for me to be here."

"Very well. You shall have your own chambers and have the freedom to come and go as you wish, but you are obligated to attend to the king whenever it pleases him."

I then looked into his eyes again. They were like sapphires.

He bowed his head, cheeks blushing. "Thank you, my queen."

I gestured for him to follow me as we walked toward the guest chambers. "So why did Zeus invite you here?"

"I am homeless, my lady," he explained, getting straight to the point. "Your husband took pity on me, and invited me to Olympos as a guest. Not that I deserve it — my offences should refuse all favours."

I glanced back at him as we passed through a set of golden doors. "How so?"

"I killed a guest of mine," he mumbled, eyes downcast, keeping his voice low as we passed some courtiers.

I stared at him, coming to a halt. "You violated the rules of hospitality?"

He nodded. "It is among the worst offences, I know, to betray the one who relies upon you for food, warmth and shelter. However, my guest was a thief before he stayed with me. He robbed some of my horses, and I was furious. So, I arranged a banquet, invited him and shoved him onto some hot coals, killing him."

"This was on impulse?" I asked, raising an eyebrow.

He shook his head, looking sorrowful. "No. To my shame, my lady, I planned it."

I began to walk again, him following. "Who was this man to you?"

Hearing silence behind me, I stopped and turned around again. "Lord Ixion?"

He pursed his lips slightly. "My father-in-law."

Admittedly, something within me fell. Disappointment, perhaps. "I see."

"So, I am a kin-slayer too," he said.

I decided to take pity on him, since my husband had. "Well, if Zeus has invited you here, he must be willing to forgive you."

"Thank you for your kind words, my lady." He glanced at me with a glimmer of hope in his eyes.

I gestured to the door down the corridor. "Your chambers are there. I shall return with hot water. Can you submit any weapons or instruments to my care?"

He shook his head, forcing a smile. "None, my lady. I have no possessions of my own."

I returned with an amphora of water and helped him wash with a rag, as was customary of a host. He needed to strip, and I did my best to avert my eyes. Although he was only mortal, I was still embarrassed. He had some scars, and minor wounds, which I helped treat, but his toned physique with strong muscles and taut skin stayed my attention. As I peeked more and more, I felt an excitement I had not experienced before. I did not know where it came from. As he did not seem shy to be bare before the Queen of Olympos, I wondered if there was really an awkward silence in the air or if it was just my imagination?

Afterwards, I bathed and washed his feet while listening to the rest of his tale: he was married to a woman called Dia. Ixion had promised a gift to her father that would be the same value as her bride price, which he never delivered upon, and so incurring the theft of his horses.

When I had finished tending to him, I sent servants to bring him food and wine. "Dinner shall be ready at sunset, but I assume you would not deny a small meal after your travels."

He smiled and shook his head, dimples in his cheeks and stars in his eyes.

My chest felt warm, and my feet felt light as I left his chambers.

At dinner, before a hall full of courtiers, he publicly thanked Zeus and me for our kindness: "Zeus has proved the most generous and benevolent of hosts and his wife the most charming and kindest of hostesses," he declared.

The room erupted into applause, for they already loved him — Ixion was handsome, charming, and charismatic.

When the chorus commenced and the Muse band played, I watched him move around the room as he mingled and danced with the other nymphs and minor goddesses. He seems so utterly sure of himself. Or maybe he felt he had nothing more to lose. Whatever it was, he was a magnet to my eyes; whenever his glance met mine, he smiled.

After some time, he approached the top table, bowed to Zeus and then to me. "My Lord Zeus. May I have your permission to dance with your wife?" he asked.

I held my breath, not quite believing how bold he had been.

Zeus, seeming pleasantly surprised at the audacious but confident question, allowed it.

Ixion thanked him sincerely, holding out his hand to me. "Of course, if it also pleases you, my lady?" He may have asked a foolish question, but he was not a fool.

It was the happiest I had ever been and the best night of my life. His hand was much larger than mine but softer than that of Zeus. He was gentle and did not pull me in any direction. Several times he asked if I was weary. Each time I insisted on another dance. He was delighted to oblige me.

"Not for the honour but for the pleasure," he said.

When most of the guests had gone, we were still whisking each other around the floor. I even caught Aphrodite looking at me as she departed on the arm of Ares. She raised an eyebrow at me. There was no malice in her face, no jealousy; instead, she seemed pleased for me.

That was when I spotted Zeus, still at the top table, glaring at us. There was no smile on his face. I knew he was wondering how and why his queen and guest had quickly become so friendly. So, I slowed down my steps and came to a halt as if to catch my breath.

"My lady?" Ixion asked, stopping and standing in front of me.

I smiled gratefully. "I think that is enough for one night."

"Of course, my lady."

Turning, I jumped to see Zeus suddenly standing there.

"I hope you enjoyed the evening, Ixion," my husband addressed him.

Ixion bowed low. "I did, my lord, immensely." He straightened.

"Good. Now, I shall escort my wife to bed."

Zeus held out his arm to me.

I froze. *Escort me where?*

"Of course, my lord." Ixion bowed his head and stepped aside. He smiled pleasantly, addressing me. "Thank you for the dance, my lady."

I nodded at him, but my throat was too tight to speak.

Zeus grabbed my hand, pulling me to his side.

I struggled to keep up as he charged from the hall. I even had to run slightly to meet his pace. As we reached my room, fear flooded me. "Zeus, why the rush —"

He kicked open the door and threw me inside.

I cried out as I stumbled. Regaining my balance, I turned to see Zeus slam the door behind him. Almost instantly, his hand was on my throat, pushing me against the wall.

"You are the one moving too fast, wife," he spat in my face, teeth bared.

"Zeus, I —" I gasped.

"I will not be made a fool of in my own home," he growled. "What is more, he is a guest."

"I am sorry," I wheezed, eyes closing as his grip tightened.

"You shall be even more sorry when I —"

But he never got to finish his threat when my bedroom door opened, and in came Ixion.

Zeus let go of me and turned around.

I sucked in a deep breath, letting the air fill my lungs.

"Oh, forgive me, my lord, my lady," Ixion gasped, eyes wide, bowing low. "I must be more lost than I thought."

"Do you require an escort?" Zeus replied sharply, his voice more of a snarl.

Ixion straightened, trying for a nervous smile. "Perhaps."

"Then allow me," Zeus grunted, approaching him. "My wife went to your chamber earlier. I must be allowed the honour too."

Ixion frowned slightly, bowing his head. "The honour is all mine, Lord Zeus."

My husband walked past him and left the room without glancing backwards.

As Ixion rushed to follow, he briefly looked my way, concerned and confused. Before he closed the door behind him, he silently mouthed, "Goodnight."

I was trembling too much to reply or even remove myself from the wall.

I did not get to bed that night. Instead, I went straight to the courtyard, ambling towards the black pool in the broken rocks beneath the willow tree. I glanced up at the stars, clustered together yet incredibly lonely.

Sitting down by the water's edge, I undid my sandals and put my feet into the dark pool. I sighed, feeling it cool my hot aching feet.

"My lady?" a familiar voice asked softly.

I turned and saw Ixion approaching, his face highlighted only by Selene.

"You should not be here," I warned him.

"Normally, I would not." He sat down beside me and put his feet straight into the water. "But I have not been able to sleep. I have been wondering if you were all right."

"I have coped with Zeus's tempers so far, but thank you for stepping in."

"You are most welcome," he replied. "Yet that is not entirely why I have sought you out."

"Oh?"

"My lady, your existence is a joke," he said, his tone emotionless.

I blinked, not quite believing I had heard him correctly. Then I scowled. What right did a mortal have to make a comment like that?

"With all due respect, of course," he added quickly. "Forgive me, but the goddess of marriage married to a treacherous, abusive brute? That is a joke. In my opinion, any husband who cannot cherish his loyal and loving wife should not be with her."

I blushed, unable to disagree. "You should not speak of your host in such a way, or seek the company of his wife so brazenly."

He shrugged. "Have I ever claimed to be good at hospitality?"

I smiled slightly, remembering his father-in-law. "No."

He nudged me gently with his elbow. "Then I shall set a new record at this rate."

I snorted in laughter, unable to hide it. But then the air grew serious as our chuckles died. "I do not love Zeus either, you should know," I confessed. "I have tried, but I cannot."

"After what I saw, I would not expect you to," he said softly.

I looked into the dark water. "Thank you. Your wife is fortunate to have a husband so understanding as you."

He scoffed. "Once, maybe. Now I am an outcast husband who killed her father. I would say she considers herself very much ashamed to be my wife. She is a wise and proud creature."

"You speak highly of her. You must miss her," I said.

He tilted his head in thought. "I appreciate her. Without her, many things would not be possible for me. However, I do not love her. I don't even miss her."

His eyes met mine. "At least not at this moment."

I felt a funny sensation in my stomach. Then my chest was suddenly pounding faster than before. I looked away from him, wondering what to say.

"Have you ever betrayed her marriage bed?" I wanted to know. For some reason, that thought came to me.

He seemed slightly taken aback. "No, my lady."

I nodded, pleased to hear it. "It is odd, but, as the goddess of marriage, I find the idea of betraying my husband reprehensible. To me, infidelity is just as repellent as my husband."

"You must be at war with yourself. Perhaps Ares has the wrong jurisdictions, then."

That made me chuckle. "He is very good at his job, Lord Ixion."

"I know," he said. "He is my father. That is why I have been able to come to Olympos as a living mortal man. My son, Pirithous, takes after him."

It occurred to me then that Ixion was my grandson. However, as I was married to my brother, the idea did not dissuade me from being drawn to him.

"Do you know what Aphrodite makes of you?" I asked, teasing him.

He grinned. "I don't think she especially cares for me. But maybe she's taking a kinder view of me recently." He raised his eyebrow at me.

I couldn't help but smile in return. However, my heart then sank, remembering all the quarrels I had with her in recent years. "Aphrodite has a philosophy: unless one finds and keeps true love, one will never be the happiest one could be. She says it is always the right path to marry the one you love, but too often, that opportunity is passed up or denied."

Then I sighed. "At any rate, she no longer consoles me about my marriage. My crimes are far more extensive and deep-running than yours, Lord Ixion. I cursed, murdered, broke hearts and destroyed the lives of many, myself among them. I do not deserve love or happiness."

I was not sure why I was saying such things to him, but it felt good to confide in him.

"Despite all that, you are not a monster, my lady. Not like your husband," he reminded me. "At least, you don't look very monstrous to me."

Then he surprised me by putting an arm around me and drawing me close. Had I not been so emotionally and physically exhausted, I might have pushed him away. It was warm and reassuring. But I found I had neither the strength nor the desire to. So, I rested my head on his shoulder, and we stayed like that for a little while, listening to the willow leaves brush up against the surface of the pool.

Thinking back on it, I cannot even remember how long Ixion was at Olympos. I know that in every waking moment, every spare thought I had was dedicated to him. Something new was happening within my heart. There was no fear for the future anymore. For the first time since I was married, I felt important. Like I meant something. Every morning I would wake up and spend ages pouring over the different colours I could wear, the various hairstyles and jewellery I had, all to make an impression on him and to catch his eye. Upon reflection, I did not need to act that way when I knew he wanted me from the moment he saw me, without a crown, rouge or finery. I could not help it. Ixion made me excited, happy, and light on my feet. Whenever I would pass him by in the palace, he would send me a wink and cast sunlight upon every shadow around me. He provided me with a source of relief when Zeus was in the room, something happy to focus on amid my husband's terror. When we were alone, Ixion would let me rant and rave about him. He was always prepared to listen.

One night, while a banquet was happening in the dining hall, he offered to escort me back to my chambers. I was not so foolish as to invite him in, and he did not suggest I should, which was a pleasant change from Zeus's gross presumptions. As we walked down the corridor, with no one around, I felt his finger brush against mine. Without thinking, my hand fell into his. I could not have imagined a more natural show of affection. Then he pulled me back, making me stop.

I will never forget his words. He said that he hoped I did not feel scared of him, like I did with Zeus, that he would be ashamed of himself if I ever did and that I could always find a trustworthy, discreet confidante in him. He said he cared about me, and for as long as he could, he would protect, comfort, and give me as much as he could afford. He told me that he would make it his new calling for what remained of his life. I thought my heart would burst. I had never felt such care. He did not say that he loved me, but the tenderness and meaning in his voice and eyes were enough to overwhelm me. No one had ever said anything remotely like that to me before. No man, no god, at any rate. I felt his arms wrap around me. Suddenly I was hugging him back. My head leant perfectly against his chest. His hand stroked the crown of my head, and his fingers ran through my hair. I had never felt safer.

I know I should not have liked him as much as I did. Ixion was an exiled king, a kin-slayer, a breaker of the rules of hospitality, and my grandson. Furthermore, my loyalty and affection should have been solely for my husband. However, despite my best efforts, I realised that Zeus would never —

could never — have those things from me, but Ixion had. Yet, Ixion never became my lover. We embraced and held hands in private, but we never even kissed. I could only dream of the other things we could do together. So, I came to know what love should be like; I knew its potential; I could see what it could become. However, I was so naive to think we would get away with it. To put it bluntly, Zeus was not the fool I was.

I had been walking alone in the gardens when I heard a familiar voice behind me, saying: "Hera?"

Turning around, I smiled at Ixion with his mischievous grin.

He gave a short bow. "I hope you are well?"

I nodded. "I am. And you?"

"I have never been better, my lady. I especially enjoyed our time together last night," he said, beaming. "Not many men can say they have lain in the bed of a goddess, never mind the queen of them all."

My smile fell from my face. *What?*

"Yet I admit I was sad to awake and see you were gone," he continued, approaching me. "I wondered if I had hurt you. Yet, as you have just said, you are fine."

"Ixion, what are you talking about? What happened last night?"

His eyes widened, and he blushed, his face confused. "My lady, for a man to be bad in bed is one thing. But to be entirely forgettable?"

"Forgive me, Ixion, if I appear muddled. You escorted me to my bedchamber. We said goodnight. That was it as far as I remember." Unless I had missed something?

His expression fell blank, even forlorn. "How can you say that after last night?" he demanded quietly, hurt entering his eyes.

"What do you mean? Nothing happened."

He scoffed. "You came to me. You opened the door and got into my bed."

Fear washed through me. *I did what?*

"We had the most amazing night of my life, at least. If it was not the same for you, then just be honest and say it." His face darkened.

I stepped away from him, taken aback. I shook my head. Annoyance and hurt filled me. I glanced at the hedges around us, the open air, and was immediately conscious that someone might be listening to our conversation. So I decided to get away from him there and then. Still, I could not do it without banishing his ridiculous realities.

"Ixion, I don't know who pushed their way into your embrace last night, but it wasn't me. We said goodnight, and that was that. So, either you slept with someone else who just looked like me, or you were only dreaming," I snapped. "Either way, leave me out of this and don't you dare tell anyone that there is an 'us' when most certainly there is not. There never could be, and after this, there will never be."

Offended and confused, I swept away from him with his shocked expression and bolted for my chambers. I slammed the door behind myself and paced my bedroom. I could not hide the deep wound within me. Ixion had lain with someone else just last night. *How could he?*

There were certain rooms in the palace of Olympos I never ventured into. Some simply had never piqued my curiosity in all my years there. So that is why Zeus did it in the dining hall. I always passed through it just across the courtyard from my chambers. He wanted me to see it and what I saw championed all the horrors I had ever inflicted, all the horrors I had ever seen.

I walked into the dining room when I stumbled across it: the sight of Ixion pinned to an enormous wooden wheel. His skin was burned, blackened and charred. It was a sight I knew well from every time Zeus struck his thunderbolt at anyone. Nails had been hammered into his wrists and through the tops of his feet to keep him in place. Blood was seeping out from each limb, and pools of it gathered on the floor. His head was hanging, almost lifeless. For one terrible moment, I thought he was dead.

I rushed towards him, dropping whatever I had been carrying. I do not remember. I grabbed his head, making him look at me. What I held before my eyes terrified me beyond anything I had ever seen. His swollen, black eye and cheek, the open wound, a gash created by some blade carved in a swipe diagonally across his face, bleeding and blinding his other eye. His lips were bruised and cut at the sides to widen his mouth. Crying out in alarm, I dropped his head, jumping back. But my heart felt a little lighter when his body shuddered and groaned. He was not gone yet.

"He will not die," a familiar voice growled as if on cue.

I jumped around to see Zeus stepping out of the shadows, a bloody dagger in his hand. I gulped, unable to speak.

"Is that not what you wanted?" Zeus hissed, approaching me, grabbing my face with one hand and yanking me towards him. "For him to be around forever?"

I winced in pain, avoiding his eyes, but his spit covered my cheek.

Zeus pushed me away, and I cried out, stumbling backwards. "Well, that is what you shall get." He moved towards Ixion.

I rushed after him. "Zeus, please. Whatever I have done, whatever he has done to offend you, I am sorry," I begged him.

He spun around and slapped me across the cheek. When his palm struck me, it felt like the world was crashing against my face.

I fell to the marble floor, my vision spun, and I could not move or focus.

Then Zeus was kneeling over me. He grabbed my throat.

I strained, unable to breathe.

"When that princeling pranced through those doors, he went after you, and you welcomed it, my dear wife," he spat. "I tricked him into thinking he was sleeping with you. It was not truly you but a shadow, a vision, a cloud even, with your face, voice, and body. He had no qualms about betraying his king. While he may not have truly taken what is mine, and while you denied it, you nevertheless cast aside the unending loyalty of your heart. This gives me grave cause for concern."

Then Zeus reached for a burning torch on the wall. Before I could guess what he was about to do, he held fire to the bottom of the wooden wheel of Ixion.

Flames engulfed the wheel instantly, turning it into a circle of fire. Ixion did not seem to comprehend what was happening until it was too late. His head was thrown back in agonised energy as the fire burned away at his skin.

I watched in horror as he was burnt alive.

His screams climbed into the air, howling with agony.

I looked away, unable to see anymore, just hoping and dreading for it to be over. My gaze landed on Zeus, at the smile of victory on his lips.

"You have a short memory, wife," he said. "Did I not say he would be around forever? But you shall never see him again, for he will burn in the depths of Tartaros for the rest of time." My stomach dropped as he raised his enormous foot and kicked the burning wheel into motion. Smashing through the archways out to the courtyard, bypassing the pool of cool water and the willow tree above it, the flaming wheel and Ixion dropped off the edge of Heaven down into the world below, destined to roll on for eternity.

All I could do was watch as Ixion disappeared from my life. Sobs and wails filled the air. Something wet was on my cheeks. Servants rushed to my side to see what the matter was. I hadn't even realised I was the one crying.

Zeus did not even stay to relish my pain.

I sat against the tree bark, dumb to the birdsong and the distant sound of a stream. After trying to chase Ixion's wheel down the mountain, I was lying among the dirt and leaves. I had been unsuccessful, obviously. So, I stared into the distance, to where I had last seen it spinning. Only Zeus knew where Ixion was now. Suddenly I heard a branch break and leaves crunch underfoot. Turning around, I saw Aphrodite standing there.

Her eyes were wide as she gazed back at me. She took a step toward me.

Shaking my head, I looked away. "Please, leave."

"I did not come to make it worse," she replied.

"I do not care," I croaked, voice hoarse. "I want to be alone."

However, her footsteps only drew nearer. "You've always told yourself things that are not true, Hera. That has always been your problem," she muttered.

I squeezed my eyes shut, the horrifying image of Ixion's burning body invading my mind again. *Please, go*, I begged her silently. However, she was not one to listen; she always knew better.

"It could be worse," she added.

I sniffled, looking at her in confusion.

"Ixion could have been here for longer. You could have loved him for longer," she said. The pity and concern were evident in her blue eyes.

I scowled. "So, am I supposed to feel grateful that I only had him for a short while? For once, I finally felt loved, but we never even kissed. All he did was let me laugh and smile and dance."

I closed my eyes. "I never thought one touch could be so gentle or that a man could be so caring. Ixion gave me a taste of what love could be like. I will never have that again."

Aphrodite took my hand, squeezing it, and said in her soft, honey-like voice: "I know, which is why I have come: to make peace with you."

I blinked, caught off guard. "What?"

"I got my justice from you the day I won the golden apple. I should have gone no further. While there is only so much that can be done about Zeus, I can at least be here for you."

I stared at her in wonder.

She smiled sadly. "May I give you some advice?"

I nodded.

"When you get up, never cry over Ixion again. You cannot afford for Zeus to see your tears or to hear them. It will only let him know that he has won. You must not give him that satisfaction."

So, we sat together, leaning on each other, backs against the tree. Aphrodite listened to me weep and let me reminisce about how Ixion's smile had caused mine, how his laughter planted mine, and how his demise brought my devastation. Then, once his loss had been mourned, she helped me up from the dirt, and we trudged back towards the palace.

I took her advice. I never cried over Ixion again. But I refused to let it go. He had shown me love, something Zeus could never do. And this time, I would not let him win. I laid in bed for several days, as I thought. I did not sleep, despite telling people I was tired. I did not eat, despite feeling hungry. I needed a plan. Soon, deep in the turmoil and the rage and the pain, I found what I needed to do.

22: MOUNT THORNAX

It had been centuries since I had been on Mount Thornax. It was still just as green, the brambles cutting across narrow pathways. It took me a relatively short time to find the cave again. When I spotted it through the tree branches, my heart plummeted into my stomach. Goosebumps crawled over my skin, and my throat ran dry. It was as if I had never left it at all.

Despite my body telling me to run, to not even look at it, I steadily took steps towards the cave. Reaching the entrance, I sat down at the edge, running my hand along floor, remembering every movement. My stomach churned. I closed my eyes, tasting the rising bile.

The sound of a bird's call overhead. My eyes flew open. But there was nothing above me except rock, towering green trees, and a blue sky. Looking around, I was alone. It was just a cave, just a forest, just a mountain. Zeus would have found a way no matter what. There was nothing to fear here.

"My lady," Athene said in surprise. "To what do I owe the pleasure?"

They gestured to a chair in the corner of the temple. "Please, sit."

I obliged, my footsteps echoing on the marble floor, and nearly collapsed into the seat. It was very comfortable. I closed my eyes, feeling myself sinking into the cushioning.

"Hera?" they asked again, softly.

I opened my eyes and took a deep breath. "I have tried everything I can think of, and nothing has worked. I have run out of ideas, and now I am running out of strength. I am not asking for your help. Zeus is your father — it would hardly be fair. I just want some advice. You are Wisdom, after all."

They shook their head, frowning as they looked down on me from where they stood. "What do you want to hear? That there is hope? Zeus can crush your whole world. He has not yet done so because he has not deemed you a serious enough threat, just someone that can be kicked back into submission if the kick is hard enough. However, that will not last if you keep this up. The wisest thing to do now would be to stop resisting him. Otherwise, you could lose everything."

I sighed. "That may be true, but I have never claimed to be wise. Athene, I still have some fight left in me, and I am determined to use it. One last time."

Athene huffed. "What do you want from Zeus?"

"I do not understand you."

"What would be an ideal outcome from all of this for you? What do you want from him?"

I blinked. Was it not obvious?

"I want it to stop. At the least, I want," I gulped, feeling my eyes sting, "respect. Care. Loyalty. I was forced into this marriage. The least my husband could do is honour me in it, consider my feelings, and be kind. I tried to be a good wife. I wanted to please him. I tended to his palace. I gave him children. I even raised those who were not mine. However, it is not just my efforts and my pain that was never acknowledged. I hate what he has made me in the eyes of others. I am the hysterical wife, the burden that pesters and restrains him from all freedoms. He has turned me into a monster.

"Yet, in a way, I also would like his good opinion. I want him to care for me. I want our marriage to work, not because I want him but because I know I will never have anyone else. However, he will never look at me in any other way than as a mule for him to breed with. If he saw me as an individual with feelings, he would have to respect me first. That will never happen. So, I will settle for a marriage that does not make me feel worthless.

"I want an apology, a genuine one, for everything. I want Zeus to regret what he has done to me. I want him to beg for my forgiveness and to try every day to deserve my cooperation and kindness. However, he would first have to care to do that, and he never will."

I stopped and shook my head. "Yet, I never want Zeus to touch me again. I never want to see him again. I never want to be anywhere near him. He is repulsive and terrifying. I can barely stand to be in the same room as him. Every instinct tells me to run when I am with him because I never know what to expect, whether it be pain or humiliation at his hands."

I took a deep breath, knowing I was about to confess my innermost feelings, ones they may not want to hear. "Most of all, I want Zeus to feel agony every day for the rest of his existence; without relief. I want him to suffer the worst kind of torture possible and never to be parted from it, just like I will never be from mine. That is what I want," I finished. It was a lot, but it was all justifiable.

Athene nodded slowly, with an expression of grief and dread on their face. "Well, there is no use in pretending you may get any of that. But all wars end, Hera. You learned that at Ilion. There is victory, defeat, surrender —"

"Which might as well be defeat," I cut in.

"Or a treaty," they finished, raising their eyebrows at me.

"A treaty?" I frowned.

They shrugged. "Why not negotiate with him? Have you tried that yet?"

"I have told him in the past what I desire. He does not care. Whenever I give an opinion or have a problem, he shoots me down," I stressed, shaking my head.

"He also does not want any more trouble than he can avoid. No one does," they stated. "You have caused him all manner of inconveniences. You say that he only perceives you as hysterical and unreasonable. He may be willing to listen to you if you explain your troubles calmly and rationally, without tears, which are famously female, and our world does not look kindly upon the female. Perhaps, if you can clearly explain to him how he would benefit, Zeus may be willing to discuss your terms and even agree to some of them."

I almost snorted in laughter, but I had enough respect for Athene's advice not to. "You are asking me to have hope in his better nature. Athene, he does not have one."

"Do not shed mortal blood or divine ichor unnecessarily until you know you have no other choice. Always prioritise peace. That should be your first course of action."

I scoffed at that. I could not hide my disappointment. I had been hoping for something more substantial. I shifted in my seat. "What if that does not work? What if he refuses?"

Athene looked away.

"I shall not surrender," I told them, shaking my head. "Not yet."

Athene nodded. Then their eyes widened, staring into the distance.

Whether their expression was one of awe or horror, I could not tell.

"Oh," they breathed. "There might be something."

"What?" I demanded.

They gazed at me for a few moments, then shook their head, pressing their lips together. "Telling you would not be protecting my father."

My face fell. "Athene."

They clasped their hands in front of them. "It will solve nearly all your problems but requires great courage and self-control," they said thoughtfully. "He would never be able to cheat again, and could not continue being your husband."

"Tell me," I begged.

"It is unspeakable, a crime against nature," they stated gravely. "It is terrible to even consider."

"Terrible?" I repeated softly. "I am an expert in the terrible."

Losing my patience with Athene, I got up from my chair, pacing around their temple, letting my thoughts override my tongue. "Did I not make Lamia eat her own children? Have I not given birth to a Gigante who then waged war upon my family? Did I not drop my own son off this very mountain? Did I not give orders for Leto to be exiled and raped? Did I not have Io chased all over the world without respite? Have I not rebelled against my own husband? Did I not force Aphrodite to get married? Did I not make Herakles slaughter his own family, torment him, and then cause his own wife to unknowingly kill him? Did I not curse Aphrodite so she would give birth to a child who could only resort to sexual assault to feel any love in his life? Did I not turn a woman into a crane, just because she had said one thing without thought? Am I not responsible for the deaths of thousands on the plains of Ilion? Did I not plague Thebes for years, first by illegally marrying their king and queen, then by harassing the city with a Sphinx? Did I not blind a man for merely having an opinion? Did I not, for no reason at all, kill two sons of my own priestess after they did their duty not just well but brilliantly? I am sure that I have done other terrible things, surpassed only by Zeus himself. Yet perhaps not even he is worse than me. Maybe I am truly the worst, most vain, jealous, rash, and evil Olympian to exist," I seethed.

Athene nodded, thoughtfully. "That is what I am betting on."

I frowned. "What are you saying?"

"That you might just be capable of it. But you would be a monster with no right to even dwell on Olympos. Any remaining pity for you would disappear entirely. You would have to act swiftly to ensure Zeus's silence. However, should you succeed, you would certainly be free from him forever."

"Then what is it? What are you talking about?"

"First, negotiate with him. If that fails, I shall tell you."

Scowling, I shook my head. "Do you not want me to be happy?"

"Yes, I do." Their voice was harsh and defensive. "Everyone wants you to be happy, Hera. However, we tried to help you before, and we failed. You are the only one left willing to stand up to Zeus. I admire your courage."

I looked away, refusing to be flattered out of my annoyance.

They shook their head, exasperated. "You just asked for my counsel. I advise that you first try to negotiate with Zeus. You have nothing to fear from him."

I blinked. "You just said that he could destroy my whole world!"

Athene approached and took my hands gently. "He could. But he could never destroy you, for you are not just his sister. You are not just some poor creature that he bullied at the right time in the right way. There is a reason the Moirai have called you the origin of all things. There is a reason that wherever you walk, the flowers bloom and the trees grow greener. There is a reason you can give birth on your own. There is a reason you care about everything so much more than anyone else. There is a reason you can control the very breath of another. Hera, you are not just what it means to be a wife, or a mother, or even female. You are so much more than that."

She left me speechless.

"At least that is what I believe," they added. "Wisdom knows to never be certain of anything."

I opened the golden doors to the throne room and went inside.

Zeus was seated at the other end, with laurels around his head. He looked tired. He cleared his throat as I approached. "What do you want, Hera?"

I stood before him now, apprehensive already.

I clasped my hands in front of me. "I come to you in hope, my lord," I told him, trying not to let my voice shake.

His chest heaved. "What hope?"

"In the hope that you will grant me a wish," I continued.

He pursed his lips. "They do not call me omnipotent for nothing, but it will depend on the nature of your demand."

I shook my head. "I make no demand, only a request. It will not require any miracles, magic, or effort."

"Then speak it."

I took a deep breath and a step closer, standing directly in front of his throne. "I hope you will agree with me when I say that we often cause each other unnecessary inconvenience," I went on softly, yet my voice still echoed around the marble hall.

He his jaw hardened. "Well, it is certainly true on your side. I cannot think what I could do to get in your way."

"Then I will stop being such a nuisance. I will cease all harm to those you take to your bed if you promise me I will never be one of them again."

He frowned. "What?"

I felt goosebumps on my arms. *Oh, Gaia, what am I saying?* I urged myself to continue. "If I never have to experience your bedchamber again."

My voice was barely audible, but he had heard me just fine.

"You mean," he said softly — but I could sense the danger in his tone — leaning his elbows on his knees, "that you would refuse to carry out the one duty a wife must? The one thing that makes a wife what she is? You, the goddess of marriage?"

There was no going back now. "All I ask is distance from your bed. I will carry out every other duty."

"Naturally." He sat back on his throne, tapping his finger on his thigh in thought.

It was not working, and every instinct told me to bolt.

His silver eyes bore into me, cold and unfeeling. Then in a low voice: "Who are you to refuse me or put limitations on me? I am your husband and your king. You have no right to reject me. You never did."

You never did. The words lit a fire in my ichor. "You once sought my affection. I am offering it, but I need some time and space first."

He rose from his throne, towering over me. "Time and space? I bend these to my will, dear wife." His voice rose with frustration. "When will you just be content in your role, as all others are? In fact, you should be grateful! You should feel nothing but pleasure and honour. You should be on your knees. I really am reaching my limit with you, Hera! I have made you the most fortunate being in the universe and you have never even thanked me," he barked, saliva flying out of his mouth. "Just get out!"

He sat back down into his throne, not looking at me.

As I bowed and turned away from him, my body was trembling. My cheeks were wet and my throat was straining against my sobs.

Then, halfway between him and the door, I stopped for a few moments, my eyes searching the air. The tears dried up. My mouth parted in realisation. I remembered Athene's words: *He would never be able to cheat again, and could not continue being your husband.*

I knew what it was, what she meant. I had it.

"Hera?" Zeus demanded from behind me.

Taking a deep breath and mustering all my willpower, I turned to face him. Slowly, I approached him. The idea had not fully formed in my mind. It was not ready. I needed time. Maybe it was madness. Maybe it would make everything so much worse, although I could not imagine how. I had to try. It was the only thing that made sense. Zeus would not be able to hurt me afterwards, in any way at all.

"You are right." I walked toward him calmly.

He blinked, caught off guard. It was not what he had expected me to say.

I reached the dais and looked up into his frown. "You always have been right. I have been selfish, conceited, and arrogant. I should have never tried to dictate you," I continued, holding his eyes in mine.

The storms were clearing, and he visibly relaxed as he realised what this was.

I climbed the few steps up to his feet, fell on my knees before him, and clasped his hands. "I am honoured to be your wife and queen. It is a blessing for which I am most indebted and grateful to you."

I bent my head, staring forlornly at the floor. "However, I know it is too late to offer you my apology or even my love."

There was a moment of silence.

"Your love?" he repeated, incredulous.

"Yes. I love you, Zeus." I nodded, raising my head to see his stunned face. "I have been too and jealous. I have let that cloud my judgement for so long. I am beyond ashamed. So, I shall not trouble you any further."

I rose as if to turn away.

"Wait, Hera," he said, grabbing my wrist and drawing me back to him as he stood up.

I sucked in a breath - our chests were nearly touching.

"Do not go," he whispered. His eyes ran over me, smiling slightly. "For you are just as beautiful as the day I first saw you."

I glanced coyly at him. "When you pulled me from our father's stomach?"

He chuckled lightly and held my hand, caressing it with his thumb. "Yes. Even then, you were gorgeous to me."

I smiled.

He raised his other hand and gently stroked my cheek. "I have loved you since that moment. I still do. All my anger and all the other women were just silly dalliances when I thought you did not love me."

"Truly?"

He nodded and ran his thumb over my lips. "Truly."

Knowing he wanted me to, I leaned in and kissed him lightly on the lips. *Again.*

He kissed me back more firmly. His hand cupped my face, tilting my head, and the other snaked around my waist as he kissed me deeper. *Yes, closer.*

I ran my hands up his chest and buried them in his golden hair.

He groaned slightly and moved his mouth to my neck.

I pulled back, giggling.

Grinning, he lent in again.

That's it.

As if they had a life of their own, my arms pushed him away, back onto his throne.

For a moment, he was surprised, but then his eyes widened when he saw me kneel.

I lifted up the hem of his tunic. I kissed his skin, slowly and lightly, my lips winding their way up his thigh. I took his member in my hand, putting my open mouth over it. I had heard of whores who did this for their clients. The thought had never appealed to me until now.

Zeus's eyes fluttered closed, his head resting on the top of the throne.

Now.

I bit down. Sharply. Tightly. My teeth took hold of all they could.

Warm ichor spurted into my mouth.

Zeus howled in agony, his voice filling the room.

I pulled back, blowing all I had taken out of my mouth, sending it flying onto the marble floor. I tried not to retch as I shot up to my feet and scooped up the remains of my husband's manhood from the floor. I looked back at him, wanting to know what my victory looked like on him..

Zeus was whimpering in pain, staring in disbelief at the growing stain of ichor on his tunic, his hands searching desperately for his mutilated part. Then he looked at me with wide, petrified eyes. "Y-you bitch! W-what have you d-done?"

He tried to take a step forward but collapsed onto his knees on the floor of the dais. Tears were streaming down his face. "I will k-kill —"

My heart hammered in my chest. "Oh no, my love. You will never touch me again."

For a brief moment I couldn't look at him. Perhaps I couldn't fathom what was happening, what I had done. I turned and spotted my reflection in a mirror on the far wall. I was spattered with his ichor. *Did I do the right thing?*

His shrieks of torment invaded my ears. I had never heard a sound more beautiful, more musical to my ears. I closed my eyes briefly, savouring it.

"I am t-the k-king!" he cried out.

I turned to face him, kneeling in a pool of ichor, and shook my head. There was so much I wanted say. I wanted to taunt him. I wanted to tell him how his reign was over, that now no man on Earth would respect him and not even the lowest of whores would touch him. I wanted to spell it out for him. But my teeth shook even as I said: "Not anymore." *You are over. You are done, husband.*

But he looked at me blankly. He didn't understand, even now. He would never be able to, I realised, never able to fathom anything less than what had been the last several centuries. He probably thought this was all a terrible dream and he would wake up shortly.

That was not good enough. Not at all.

My hand that was holding his member, holding it so tight I thought I could pierce it even with my nails, let go of its grip. I lunged at Zeus. He would not wake up. Whatever his perception, this would be the end of it.

I grabbed his throat with my hands, squeezing with all my strength. I yanked the air from his lungs and let no more in. I put all my remaining anger into my strength, and let my husband, my baby brother, perish.

His eyes bulged from their sockets. The veins in his neck turned blue, and his cheeks slowly went purple as he choked. If he hadn't been so wounded, perhaps he would have been strong enough to break away. But he was broken. Gradually, his kicks slowed as he weakened, and his eyes glazed over. At last, he was still, his soul trapped inside a body that could not function. He had never looked more like our father.

23: CHERA

I closed my eyes for a few minutes. My head couldn't decide if it was at peace or in chaos. Then the tears started to come. I had just ended his life, practically, my baby brother's life. I had taken his manhood and ended his life. Among my crimes, it was hardly the worst. But it meant more. And it had been so quick, almost easy. Was that it? It couldn't be. He was finished but that didn't mean I was. We were gods. We had no end. I would never end. But what now? Finally, it was for me to decide. I opened my eyes and saw the dais.

"You can hear me, can you not?" I whispered, turning around to him. "Maybe you can still see too. Can you see this?"

Angling Zeus's face towards the dais, I got to my feet and picked up his crown from the pool of ichor on the floor. I wiped it dry on his tunic, walked to his throne, and, facing him, staring blankly back at me, I sat down in his place and placed the crown on my head.

I relaxed into it and sighed. I looked out onto the empty hall from my perch on high, empty save for his body before my feet. I gripped the golden armrests. So, this is what it felt like to rule the world. No, not just the world. The cosmos.

Then I frowned. "You know, this seat is really uncomfortable," I remarked, standing up. "No wonder you were so awful all the time."

Raising my foot, I kicked his throne down the steps of the dais. It was heavy, but I managed. It narrowly missed my husband as it clattered over him.

I grabbed my throne from the other side of dais and moved it into the centre. I settled down into it, this time able to savour my victory the better. My eyes felt heavy.

I sighed, happily. "This is nice, isn't it?"

I glanced down at Zeus. "You are probably shocked. All those prophecies saying you would be overthrown by your son."

I leaned forward on my knees, looking down into his eyes. "But I got tired of waiting for one of them to do it, I suppose. You know, I tried to make you happy. I wanted you to see my worth, but I always seemed to fail."

I pursed my lips in thought. "I failed because you deceived me. Yes. You lied to me. You said you cared. That made me assume you cared for others. What a waste it all was — trying to hurt you by hurting those I believed you loved. It took me too long to understand that you were incapable of love. I thought you meant your wedding vows when you promised to cherish and protect me, but you betrayed that promise every day. Now, you cannot even fulfil your duty as a husband. So, our match is void, is it not? As the authority on such matters, I would say that a lack of ability to procreate is a sufficient reason to divorce. Would you not agree, my love?"

I sighed, pondering out loud. "I wonder: shall they call me a widow now? *Chera*? I cannot say. One day, perhaps, I shall marry again. Although, that is now no longer your concern. The important thing, I think, for us both to take from all of this is that rulers cannot always do what they please. One must look after one's subjects, not mistreat them. Because you see, my dear, there is no ruler without the ruled. For all your intelligence and cunning, I don't think you ever really figured that one out."

I glared at him. "I thought it was my fault — that day in the cave. I made excuses for you, telling myself that if I had accepted your marriage proposal in the first place, it would not have happened. So, I convinced myself you would be good to me if I married you, that you will be satisfied when you finally get what you asked for. Alas, no. What a naive fool I was, and how ingenious you were to get me to blame myself for your decisions and your behaviour!" I jabbed a finger in his face.

He stayed silent, of course, unable to reply.

I snorted in laughter. "It must have been so embarrassing for you, the ruler of the world, handsome, young, virile, and yet not even your own sister would have you. I understand. You were hurt and ashamed. You wanted to show me you were in charge. However, I think you also just wanted to feel wanted. Or were you so used to getting your way that you simply decided to take what you could, like a child, without thinking of what it would do to me? I think now that it was a mixture of all of that: insecurity, immaturity, and anger. You wanted an adoring, devoted wife who would worship you without hesitation, who would be a living confirmation of everything you believed about yourself. But you did not get it, not from me anyway."

I leaned forward, until my face was nearly touching his. "However, if you think for one moment that raping her, forcing her to be yours, could have achieved that love, you are an idiot."

Part of me almost wished I had not taken away his ability to respond or make expressions — I would have liked to see his reaction.

"Do you have any idea how little any of your mistresses actually wanted you? They could hardly say no. Otherwise, they would have faced your wrath as I did. How many of them forced themselves to endure your embrace to avoid your fist? Believe me when I say that you will never be truly loved by anyone, mortal or divine."

I shook my head, my lower lip curling in distaste at the sight of him. "You refused to take no for an answer, unable to accept the desires of others if they did not suit yours, and utterly incompetent at controlling your anger. It was pathetic."

I took a deep breath, trying to calm myself. I leaned back in my throne. "Despite everything I have ever done, I am never more ashamed than when I accepted you as my husband. It was my weakest, lowest moment. My worst decision was to marry you. Yours was to underestimate me."

The doors to the throne room opened as the Olympian court streamed into their assembly room, for this was the usual time Zeus called the court to gather. Gasps of horror and shock sounded throughout the hall. They looked from me to Zeus and back again, not believing, not knowing what to think or say.

Athene hurried forward, knelt by Zeus's side, and felt for his pulse, staring at his open eyes, ichor-soaked tunic, the golden pools on the floor, and the discarded member by his side. Whether they were impressed or not, I did not know. They shook their head in silent wonder.

Cautiously, Aphrodite approached me.

"Hera, what have you done?" she whispered, terror evident in her trembling voice.

"I am claiming my birthright," I said firmly, claiming my authority.

She shook her head. "You have killed the king."

"As much as possible, yes. His soul is still inside, looking out."

I looked at the rest of the court. "Shocking that a wife could do such a thing. Yet, tell me truthfully, do any of you truly mourn the end of Zeus's reign?"

The hall remained silent. Everyone looked at each other. They bowed their heads.

"Kneel," I commanded. "Or face his fate."

Aphrodite's face grew pale, and Athene looked up at me in alarm. The room was still; no one moved. I glared at Aphrodite. Slowly, she descended onto her knees in front of the dais. Athene stared at her from behind, in shock, and then at me in despair. Then they did the same, and the rest of the court followed suit.

One by one, every Olympian courtier bowed before me.

Gazing upon them all, cowering in fear, looking back at me with hatred in their eyes, I realised that whatever Zeus had enjoyed from this position, I did not share. My heart began to beat fast again. I saw his body on the floor, all that I had done. More fear. More hatred. More loneliness. That's not what I was seeking. So, I sighed and took the crown off my head and stood up.

People looked at me murmuring, and I did not move anymore, conscious of what could happen when I got down from the dais. I still had a chance to make something good out of this, did I not? I never imagined I would get this far, actually getting rid of Zeus. But simply because my mind changed too frequently did not mean I couldn't create something steady and reliable.

"Long ago," I spoke, "when Olympos was first built, the Kronides promised a democracy. It never happened. They overthrew one tyranny to replace it with another. So, my first and only act as ruler of Olympos is to establish a council of the gods to whom all final decisions will be made by passing majority votes. The assemblies will remain in place. However, instead of having a single monarch, Olympos will have many, all ruling together as equals."

Then I glanced at the nymphs lining the walls and gestured to Zeus. "Get him out of my sight. Send him to Haides. He will know what to do."

There was no shortage of volunteers to send Zeus to his darkened destiny. The courtiers were happy to oblige. It was the last time I ever laid eyes on what remained of him. It would be too soon if I ever did again in my eternal life.

With that, my reign ended as quickly as it had begun.

24: PARTHENOS

Athene and I were sitting in the courtyard, looking out on Hellas, our feet in the pool below the willow tree, basking under Helios's intense light — he was shining brighter now that he was free to shine as he wanted.

"I never believed you would go through with it," they said beside me. "The actual killing bit, I mean. The maiming I expected. Removing his manhood is not just of functional importance to you but a significant signal to the world. The killing was ... terrible."

"It was. Have I not done other terrible things?" I replied quietly, gazing out onto the green view. I had an eternity to wonder if I had truly released myself and if I had done it in the right way.

"I suppose," they mumbled. "At least you are free now."

I looked down at my hands. They were trembling.

Athene took them gently in their lap and massaged them. "A condition of pain is that we often unwittingly elicit it in others. It is a disease."

"How do I get rid of it?" I whispered.

"Renewal, and this is the perfect time to do it."

I glanced at them. "What do you mean?"

Athene sighed and nodded to the willow tree across the courtyard. "It is springtime, Hera. The season of birth and rebirth."

I was lost.

They rolled their eyes slightly. "Obviously, what has passed can never be reversed, but you do not have to continue like this. Do not forget what has happened but do not dwell on it either. Every spring, restart. Revirginise yourself. Become a maiden again, a parthenos."

I nodded, willing to try. "How?"

They shrugged, smiling. "It is not fixed for everyone. The ritual is what will feel right for you at the time. Do not doubt yourself."

I heeded their advice. I travelled far and wide throughout Hellas to find the perfect place for my rebirth. I felt I would know when I saw it. And I did.

It was the Kanathos spring at Nauplia. Sunset was casting its warm golden glow over the watery surface. Slowly, I took off my crown, placing it on a rock and letting my hair loose. Then I removed my dress, dropping it to my ankles and kicking it aside. Covered only by the sun's warmth, I approached the pool and stepped inside. The water was refreshing, a cool tickle of rejuvenation. I plunged down without hesitation, submerging myself.

Opening my eyes, everything was crystal clear. I could see the detail of the rocks around me and some emerald plant life beginning to form in the crevices. I let my past be washed away, my sins, guilt, and pain. As the numbness embraced me, I knew it was complete. I rose from the water, feeling as good as new, and that was enough.

A new age dawned on Hellas. The Olympians formed a new council within the court, endeavouring to discuss matters of the kingdom and to make unanimous decisions. One of the first decisions was to create the Heraean Games, in my honour: an athletic event like the Olympics but for women. Athene and Ares took part most avidly in the new administration.

However, politics did not suit me. I attended every council meeting and contributed as much as was appropriate for a goddess of marriage and motherhood. I was still the lady in charge of the palace and, with Hestia, oversaw its management. Yet I spent most of my time at the Garden of the Hesperides, eating golden apples, lying under the Tree of Life, staring up at Nyx above. I invited Rhea and Gaia there often, where we would reminisce about the past and dream of the future. On Olympos, I went to the library some days and read scrolls concerning medicine and science's latest philosophy. I learned the lyre with the Muses and toured Earth to inspect royal marriages far and wide, ensuring they were stable and the couple content. Most of all, I always looked forward to being in the nursery, caring for the latest addition to my growing family of grandchildren and great-grandchildren.

My family wanted to give me a title. They offered to call me a queen as I had been married to a king, but I refused — I did not want to be connected to Zeus in any way. Then they suggested 'Mother of the Realm' and I agreed. Why shouldn't I?

Now you finally know the truth. So, shall you claim to not have done the same as me?

A NOTE TO THE READER

Dear Reader,

I hope you enjoyed reading this book as much as I enjoyed writing it.

This is the final book in the trilogy, so it completes my retelling of Hera's story. However, it is by no means the end of Hera, what she signifies for us individually and how seeing her in different lights can be useful.

As reviews greatly help authors starting out, please leave a rating and review on **Amazon** and **Goodreads**. You can find me **on Instagram** and **X (Twitter)**.

I sincerely hope you enjoyed this series!

Ava

Sapere Books is an exciting new publisher of brilliant fiction and popular history.

To find out more about our latest releases and our monthly bargain books visit our website:
saperebooks.com